SORROWS TO THE STONE

Harvey Sagar

Published by Harvey Sagar
ISBN: 978-1-9998573-0-1
Copyright 2017. All rights reserved
www.harveysagar.com

Preface

This book is a work of fiction. The author does not claim any veracity for statements made or the events recounted and does not claim any adherence to any of the specific opinions expressed.

Any resemblance between characters in this book and persons past or living or between events related and real-life events is purely coincidental.

Titus Andronicus Act 3 Scene 1
William Shakespeare

Therefore I tell my sorrows to the stones;
Who, though they cannot answer my distress,
Yet in some sort they are better than the tribunes,
For that they will not intercept my tale:
When I do weep, they humbly at my feet
Receive my tears and seem to weep with me;
And, were they but attired in grave weeds,
Rome could afford no tribune like to these.
A stone is soft as wax, tribunes more hard than stones;
A stone is silent, and offendeth not,
And tribunes with their tongues doom men to death.

Chapter 1

My dear sister,

How well you know me! Yes, I was responsible for that headline. Did you ask because you were impressed with its poetic quality, its shock tactics or, dare I suggest, because you thought it better than most of my efforts?

Most people to whom I have spoken are polite but imply that it is rubbish! However, I thought quite hard about it. The original was "Burnt body baffles police" but I changed it to "The strange case of a charred body, a necklace and a stone" when our new editor told me. I could have a double-line headline and, anyway, the original was more suited to one of our tabloid cousins!

No, I do not know much more about it all than appeared in my article but, if you are interested, I will keep you posted. The police are indeed baffled, not only because there are no combustibles around to suggest it was suicide but also because there are no suspects; they cannot even identify the body. All they have is the necklace.

By the way, the stone has gone missing.

Your loving brother,

Julian

Chapter 2

"Come in," said the tall, broad-shouldered, black man at the door. His outlook was benign with a half smile, deep brown eyes and open-armed gesture. "I am Adedayo. I will look after you." He led the way and she followed, through the narrow hallway, whose walls were decorated with wallpaper that was once light cream with a yellow flowered border but was now speckled with dirty brown damp patches, interspersed with fine outgrowths of green mould.

She followed him up the narrow staircase edged by a cheap, wooden bannister covered in flaking varnish. As she walked round the one-hundred-and-eighty-degree bend at the top of the staircase leading onto the landing that led to the second floor, she stopped by a small icon on the wall, dedicated to the Nigerian Yoruba god, Shango. She heard noises. She concentrated. A woman's voice crying, a man's voice grunting and a second man's voice jeering.

"This way," said Adedayo hastily, whilst beckoning her firmly with his outstretched hand. "Up the stairs."

She followed. He led her onto the upper floor and turned the light onto a room about ten feet by six. In the middle, was a double bed. By the wall, was a low table, on which was a large Victorian ceramic bowl and a cheap modern pottery jug full of water. As she passed through the door, a cockroach scurried beneath the skirting board that was buckling up from the wooden floorboards.

"This is your room," said Adedayo, gazing without emotion into her eyes, "where you can relax." After a few seconds, he added: "And where you will work." He turned away from her to leave but she stopped him.

"Please! What work am I to do?"

"What were you told?"

"They told me that I would stay in your house and you would find me work and that I would pay for my keep from the money that I earned. They could not say exactly what work it would be because it would depend on what was available when I got here. But they said that you had many contacts and there was no doubt that you would find me enough work to pay my way and more besides."

"Do you have any money?"

"My family in Nigeria has some money and I brought enough with me to, well, to deal with some problems I have. But I do not have enough to pay for rent, food and so on as well."

"I was given some money by…" She paused, then continued, "…by someone back home but that was to pay for my airfare here."

"So work is important to you?"

"Oh yes," she said, "I will not be able to live here without it. And I have to live here for some time, I am not sure how long."

"We will bring the work to you," he said, "meanwhile settle in." With a smile, he turned and walked back down the corridor.

She put her canvas bag on the floor beneath the window and sat on the bed. Light from the window fell on the ageing eiderdown beside her but stains on the window broke up the sun's rays to create a dappled effect, somehow unpleasant. After a few minutes, she began to empty the contents of her luggage into a wardrobe between the window and the corner of the room away from the door. Her silent solitude was interrupted intermittently by the recurrent, now faint, cries of the woman from the floor below.

Muonasa arranged her clothes as neatly as she could in the small space of the wardrobe and a single bedside cabinet. She put her hand into the side pocket of her bag and removed a stone, oval in shape, about the size of the palm of her hand. The stone was a uniform beige, decorated around the edge with tiny black and red stylised heads. Muonasa stared at the stone for a minute or two before closing her eyes and letting her mind wander. On this occasion, no new thoughts appeared. A little disappointed, she opened her eyes and placed the stone delicately at the base of a small wooden lamp on the bedside table and removed the remainder of her belongings from the bag. She placed a small leather pouch on the table next to the stone.

When she had finished unpacking, she moved to the window and looked through the few patches in the glass that were not obscured by grime, dust and grease. On the narrow street below, a wizened man with bent posture, shaggy beard, ragged raincoat and stumbling gait passed beneath. In his hand was a bottle. She looked to the left; a taxi drew up at the end of the street and a black woman got out. Without getting out of the car, the driver signalled through the window the destination of his passenger, in short the building from which she gazed. She strode off purposefully towards Muonasa's new home. She had a cloth wrapped around her head and was wearing a loose, long-sleeved blouse and a wrap-around skirt. She was obviously Nigerian. *Maybe a new resident, like me,* thought Muonasa.

Muonasa looked to the right. Two houses down, the road was blocked by a concrete wall, newly and amateurishly built. The bricks were unevenly stacked; the binding cement was adorned with excrescences; and the line of the top from left to right was sinusoidal. Beyond the wall was a factory unit that looked deserted except for a single, large, black BMW parked in the otherwise empty car park.

The taxi passenger strutted elegantly down the cul-de-sac and arrived at the door of Muonasa's new home. She hammered the knuckles of her right hand onto the wooden door - no bell, no knocker. She looked up and saw a small circular glass window just above the line of her eyesight. She gazed into it. By several minutes later, whilst waiting for a response, she was staring at the floor. She looked absent-mindedly to her right, to a cylindrical plastic tube lying on the barren earth. It was dirty and heavily weathered. Six inches to its right was the point of a needle; the remainder was hidden in earth.

Muonasa's attention was focussed by the creaking noise of the front door that she recognised from her own arrival not long before. She looked down as the door opened to see the muscular shoulders of her landlord and employer just protruding into her line of sight. Her fellow Nigerian passed through and the door closed.

On the floor below, another door opened. Two men walked out, slammed the door and descended the stairs. The landlord pushed his new arrival to one side as he took his money and let the men leave. They smiled; he nodded. Muonasa was listening; the voice she had heard crying now seemed to be sobbing.

Fatigue from her journey was now beginning to well up within her. She lay on the bed, which surprised her with its comfort, given the basic state of the rest of the room. Within a few minutes, her mind had shut down all attempts to rationalise what she had seen and she went to sleep. When she awoke, there was no sign of the other Nigerian girl. *Like me, taken to her room, I suppose,* thought Muonasa; *maybe she will be working here too and I can get to be friends with her.* But, in truth, despite living in the same house, Muonasa never saw her again after that day.

Following the initial trauma of the day before, the next day, her first full day in her new English home, was pleasant and settling. After eight hours' sleep, she was roused by her landlord, who brought her a plate of sausages, mashed potato and runner beans on an old, wooden tray. He explained that there was insufficient room in the house for all the inhabitants to eat together and most would have to eat in their rooms. However, a kitchen was available for communal use. He also explained that there was, of course, a toilet and also a bathroom but most of the people there, especially the women, preferred to freshen up at intervals within their own room, hence the jug and bowl. He suggested that she eat plenty and have a good night's rest. What she did not know then was that, apart from her landlord, all the occupants of the house were women.

He doubted that she needed to work the following day so she could spend a day adjusting to her new surroundings and exploring the area and get to know her way about. He pointed through the window to some sights in which she may be interested, including the church and the hotel district beyond. He felt confident that she would be able to start earning money within the next few days and he would keep her informed about the plans. She felt reassured.

Muonasa spent most of the next morning lying on her bed, consciously adjusting to her new home, even though she still did not know exactly what would be in wait for her. She knew she had to work and, yes, Adedayo had assured her that work would be available, so that was good. She also knew that she had other tasks to fulfil but all that could be dealt with in its own time.

After a sandwich lunch, brought to her by her landlord, she took his advice and ventured out of the house to explore the area. In so many ways, her new environment was no different from that of her home town in Nigeria: people living normal days, going about their business, working, relaxing and, no doubt, settling into their own homes when the light faded in the evening. People across the world are all so similar, she thought; they have the same ideals, the same concerns and the same ways of adapting to their own environment. But, of course, the superficial details were different: the architecture, the hairstyles, the dress, even the weather.

She passed by a church. Even the faiths spread across continents, she thought. Even though again the buildings were of a different design from those that she had been used to, she felt confident that the faith and the worship of those contained within them would be little different from those of the churches she knew back home.

She felt pleased that she had taken the step to travel to another continent and to find that the essence of her life was reproduced in a country so far away. Hopefully, she would be able to find friends here who shared her interests and would be able to lead a fulfilling life during her stay, even though she knew she had problems to resolve while she was here. She must not forget the primary reason for her visit.

After a couple of hours wandering, she returned to the house. Still tired from her journey the previous day, she slept on the bed for a couple of hours, dreaming of a Nigerian man in a white hat and red and white necklace, advising her of the necessary course of action to achieve fulfilment in this life. She awoke with a smile and, even though her accommodation was less than ideal, felt happy that she was where she was. She spent the evening reading the rest of a book on English tradition that she had taken for the journey and went to sleep.

Muonasa awoke at about 5 a.m., two hours earlier than her usual time. For once, she seemed to be surrounded by silence; her mind was empty and her body ached. Just one day of her so-called work had passed and she could not even switch on her mind to take on an image of what a second may bring. How many had there been? Probably only four or five but it seemed like three or four times as many. And no doubt that was her initiation day. She could expect to accommodate many more in the days to come.

She concentrated. Now she was getting some mental images: Adedayo appearing at the door, barely for long enough to announce that her work was to start that day, as he had promised, before a second man, up to now hidden by the half-open door, appeared from behind. A white man, aged about forty-five, six feet tall with an almost bald head and stubble beard. Overweight. Dressed in track pants and a hoodie. Still half hidden by the door, he was smiling - no, leering - at her from behind Adedayo's left shoulder.

Adedayo said that her job was entertainment. She was to do everything that his client requested. The client would report back to Adedayo his satisfaction or otherwise with the job she had done and he wanted her to know that her continued presence in the house was dependent on consistent good reports. On this occasion, her dress would do but he would talk over with her later what he would like her to wear for future clients. Her vision misted and her body felt to be slipping downwards into the floorboards. He did not need to say any more. Her future spelt itself out in her mind in an instant. She managed to glance across to her stone on the bedside table and wished that she could have even a few minutes more with it but there was no time. Adedayo handed the man a condom, turned and left.

A few minutes after the stranger had left, Adedayo returned with a jug of cold water, placed it on the earthenware bowl and instructed her to clean herself up and wait for the next client.

As he left, Muonasa reached for her stone, held it in the palm of her left hand and stared into it. As usual, she let her mind wander into the deeper reaches of some land that she had never known before becoming the object's owner but which she was learning to explore and understand with ever greater involvement. Even though she had now closed her eyes, she could see with clarity a green pastured land against a backdrop of a reddened sky. In the distance, against the horizon, were African huts gathered together into a small community. Men and women were milling around in their everyday domestic tasks.

She focussed her attention on the middle of the township when, as she had learned to expect, she heard a voice calling her by name. She knew that no-one else could hear it, not least because the voice had told her so. Fear not, it told her; all will be well. All she had to do was see things through and, at the end, paradise would be waiting. She would be free of her disease, free of her malevolent spirit and would be blessed with all the qualities necessary for peace and joy in this world and the next. Muonasa relaxed her taut body muscles, exhaled deeply and open her eyes. Yes, the stone was her friend. It did indeed make her feel better, as she had been promised. At least now, she could carry on, however distasteful she found her new road to freedom. Fortunately, these were the lasting memories of her first day at work.

Chapter 3

"Dr. Haynes will see you now."

She rose from her chair and followed the nurse through the waiting room area, into the corridor and down to the third door on the right, situated between two framed prints of impressionist art. The nurse held the door open to let her pass through. Muonasa, wearing her traditional Nigerian costume, walked towards the doctor seated at the far end of the room and hunched over a desk, scribbling on some notes.

"Good morning, Ms. Ajayi" said Dr. Haynes. "Do sit down. You have made a private consultation, which is fine, but sadly I do not have any information from your general practitioner or indeed anyone else. Therefore, I rely on you to inform me all about yourself. I gather that you are new to this country. Where did you come from?"

" Iree, in Nigeria."

"Tell me what's on your mind."

"A lot, to be honest."

"Let's start with the beginning."

"I don't know where it begins, where I begin."

"Then tell me something, anything."

"I have come to you to be cured of a disease I acquired in Nigeria. A doctor I saw there said that it was affecting my mind and that eventually I would go insane."

"Did he tell you the nature of this disease? Did he give it a name?"

"No."

"What else did he tell you about it?"

The leering face, the wide eyes, the certainty in his voice. The domination. In her heart, she knew, on that now seemingly distant day, that he did not make sense and he gave no justification or authority for his predictions. So why did she accept them? Again the domination - not expressed, nothing spoken, no threatening movements - just there. And still there.

"He said that I would end up crawling across the floor, unable to look after myself, constantly dribbling saliva and being unable to control my bladder or my bowels. My eyes would be fixed open wide and I would see terrifying images of supernatural beasts and giant insects crawling over the walls of my bedroom. Even if they left, I would be unable to sleep for fear that these creatures would return. And eventually, sooner or later, they would return. And probably sooner rather than later. He said my limbs would burn with an evil fire; my fingers and toes would be fixed in grotesque postures; my hearing would be replaced by a constant ringing and my taste buds would yield only pungent, acrid and acidic sensations."

"Who told you this?" asked Dr. Haynes in undisguised astonishment. "Where did you consult this doctor?"

"In the countryside. He practised traditional Nigerian medicine."

"I see. But he told you to come here?"

"Yes, he said that he did not have the means to deal with such a 'complicated disorder', as he put it, and that only a specialist in the West, preferably Great Britain, could realistically help me."

"And he said that the specialist to consult should be a psychiatrist?"

"Not in so many words but he said that I should see someone who could cure my diseased mind and I interpreted that to be a psychiatrist."

The doctor paused briefly and then continued: "What was it took you to see him in the first place?"

"I had a worry that I was losing contact with my family, my brother in particular. Then, I kept getting terrible rushes of fear that something awful was going to happen. I kept imagining one or other of them in some form of terrible accident. Sometimes I felt that I could even see and hear the accidents happening. These feelings became so frequent and so intense that eventually I just knew a disaster was about to occur."

"To whom?"

"It varied. Sometimes it was my mother, sometimes my father. And sometimes me."

"But not your brother?"

"No."

Dr. Haynes frowned, tightened his mouth, looked towards the corner of the room, leaned back in his chair and sighed. The vividness of the words that she had used to describe what would happen to her and which ostensibly stemmed from a folklore practitioner in Nigeria were striking, to say the least. They seemed to be still ringing in his ears. And the intensity of the fears for her family. Even after just a brief conversation, he admitted to himself that he was stunned. *Where to begin?* Not often these days, he thought, did he see cases potentially so involved and with such little background information to go on. Should he just tell her he is not the best person for her to see and discharge her from the clinic? But she would ask for the name of someone else and, in truth, he could not think of anyone who was likely to be as accommodating as him. *Stick with it; she needs help; start with the basics and move on methodically.*

"As far as you know, is your general health good? Have you had occasion to see a doctor about any physical complaint in, say, the last three years?"

"No."

"Were you born in Nigeria? Have you always lived there?"

"Yes."

"Have you ever been out of the country - before now?"

"No."

"Tell me about your childhood, your upbringing and your family'"

"I suppose by the standard of many people in Nigeria, we were relatively well off. My father has been manager of a quality retail clothes shop for many years. My mother does not work. My brother now works in the oil industry. We were mostly a happy family, doing most of the ordinary things that families do".

"The Church has always been very important to both my parents. My father, in particular, devotes as much time as he can to activities of the Church. My brother followed in our father's footsteps so that he too is very keenly involved. In fact, he is even more devout than my father. He prays at least three times per day."

"And do you share their views?"

"Yes, but not so rigidly. I think I am a good Anglican Christian but I studied agricultural science at college and I think that has made me a bit more open-minded."

"Do you work in that field now?"

"No. Although my father was supportive when I said I wanted to study science, he resisted when I started looking for jobs in that field. He said that it was contrary to Christ's teaching and the will of God. He said that science was out to destroy the Christian faith. To be honest, I think he was influenced a lot by my brother who never loses any opportunity to pronounce those views. In fact, he says that scientists are evil and the world would be a better place without them."

"Strong views indeed! Does he think the same about doctors?" He managed a brief half-smile.

"No - and that's the hypocrisy in him and many people like him. He realises that modern medicine - and agriculture, my field and, for that matter, the oil industry too - are increasingly dependent on the findings from science but he ignores that fact because he realises that he needs what it can offer. Sorry, perhaps I shouldn't speak like that about my brother. To be fair, he would always first consult someone more steeped in traditional African medicine but luckily, so far, he has not needed to."

"Is that why you consulted a traditional doctor in the first instance for your problems?"

"Possibly, yes. I hadn't really thought about that."

"What sort of relationship do you have with your parents and your brother?"

"My mother is wonderful and loving. I adore her. I love my father and brother too but they both like to be in control. I can take that from my father because he is my father but my brother has no right to tell me what to do but he does. And, for some reason, my father just accepts it."

"Has your brother always been like this? Is he older than you?"

"Yes, he is three years older. He has been worse since he got more involved with the church."

"Do you work now?"

"I assist my father in his store."

"So, judging by what you say, your family still live in Nigeria?"

"Yes. They still live in the same area where they were born and brought up. Except my brother - he moved to London with his job last year."

"To London! So you are both in the same city! Have you seen your brother since you arrived here?"

"No, but then I haven't made much attempt to do so. I seem to have been very busy."

"And him. Has he contacted you? I presume he knew you were coming."

"Well, he did. But he doesn't know all the details. In fact, he doesn't really know much about why I am here. I told him I had to come for treatment and maybe I would see him while I am in London but he is pretty absorbed in his own lifestyle - work, church and so on. To tell you the truth, I think he is not all that interested in anyone who does not conform to his pattern of life, even his own sister."

"Was he ever aggressive towards you?"

"Most of the time, when we were growing up, he behaved like a brother and was often kind. He was a lovely boy. But, as I said, he usually managed to make his feelings clear, especially as he got older and he could be horribly mean if I disagreed with him."

"So, if I understand correctly, the essence is that you have come here because a country doctor in Nigeria has told you that you have an illness that will lead to a horrific disturbance of your mind and body and that can only be treated here; you were brought up in a fairly well off family; and you have had a mixed relationship with your family, particularly your father and, even more so, your brother. You consulted this doctor because you were concerned about those relationships. Is that correct?"

"I think your summary is very good."

"I remain concerned and intrigued as to what kind of emotion you must have experienced to motivate you to travel to a distant country on the basis of the opinion of a single person, however meaningful he sounded. I know you said that your brother might have approved of your consulting someone steeped in traditional Nigerian medical practice but are you sure that is true? And, if I may say so, given what you have told me about the relationship with your brother, would that opinion have influenced you greatly? Could there be anything else that drew you to this person?"

"I suppose you are right. Maybe he wouldn't have approved and perhaps I am trying to rationalise everything. Maybe even trying to find a way to please my brother but I will leave that to you to judge. The truth is I don't really know what led me to this person in the country. It just seemed as if I was led there, as if it was the right thing to do."

"You were just led there?"

"Yes."

"Well, you speak very clearly, Ms. Ajayi and your English is excellent! You have explained yourself very well."

"Well, English is the official language of the country. I think it goes back to colonial times. And I also have the benefit of an education."

Dr. Haynes coughed in embarrassment. "Yes, quite. Moving on, would it be fair so say that you have, shall we say, a love-hate relationship with your brother?"

"Well, I'd say he has a love-hate relationship with me."

As the interview continued, Mark Haynes became increasingly absorbed in the potential ramifications of everything that the Nigerian told him. Psychologically intriguing, certainly, but also almost surreal. What kind of community did she live in back home? What kind of a person was her brother and what influence did he have over her? Most perplexingly, quite why had she travelled to London to seek treatment for something which he had barely even begun to define? What on earth was the Nigerian doctor referring to in his wild displays of colourful language that he used to describe her condition? What kind of illness could not be treated nearer home, even in Nigeria, which these days could hardly be described as undeveloped? He understood the words that she had spoken to him well enough but the coordinating thread of logic and rationale remained elusive.

One thing was clear: he was now too involved, too fascinated, to let his patient go. Even from a purely academic perspective, it was gripping. But there was the emotional element too; something was influencing this girl's mind. He had to find out what.

For her part, the doctor's approach was one quite unfamiliar to her. Rarely, even given the short time that she had known him, had she felt that she had found someone who was capable of identifying issues relevant to her welfare, who was obviously interested in her and was concerned and empathetic. At least, she had never experienced these qualities together in one person and without an overriding air of judgement. She knew she had made the right decision in coming here, despite its complications. She would do whatever Dr. Haynes asked her to do, would see it through and come out with fulfilment at the end; of that she was certain.

"Well, Ms. Ajayi, I now have the psychologist's report. I hope you did not find the tests too taxing," said Dr. Haynes. "Following what we discussed at our last meeting, I asked for the English versions of the tests to be given because I understand that is your principle language. Was I right in that decision? Were you comfortable with the tests?"

"The language was not a problem," said Muonasa. "I do speak Yoruba, which is also a language from where I come from, but English is better."

"Good," said the doctor. "In any case, I am not sure that the tests have been translated into Yoruba!" He smiled.

"Probably not," said Muonasa. "And, if they were, I doubt anybody would use them."

As Dr. Haynes paused to look over the test results, she continued: "Some of the questions were difficult for me to answer properly. For example, there was one asking me if I would try to get into the movies without paying but I never go to the movies."

"No, I understand. Rarely are all of the questions applicable but we ask you to imagine how you would respond if you found yourself in that situation. Did the psychologist make that clear before you started?"

"Yes, thank you."

"That particular test is just to get an overall view of your personality. There are no right or wrong answers. It helps me to know what sort of a person you are, what are your strengths and weaknesses."

After a further pause, while Dr. Haynes was scanning the results, she added: "'A minister can cure disease by praying and putting his hand on your head.' I liked that one."

"Yes, you indicated in the test that you agree strongly with that particular statement. However, the individual answers are not in themselves important. It is the pattern of answers across the whole test that really paints the picture. But, as a matter of interest, why do you single out that particular question?"

"Well, I suppose I do agree with it in one sense but, in another, I don't. I believe that there are two parts to a person, the physical and the spiritual. All aspects of a person's being are influenced by the two sides, acting together or sometimes against each other. Even in what seems to be a purely physical illness, there is a spiritual component. A doctor can deal with the physical bit but a minister is necessary for the spiritual part."

"Does that apply to mental illness as well?"

"Yes. The mind is part of the brain but is also part of the spirit."

"Well, I must congratulate you on the depth of your analysis, Ms. Ajayi," said the doctor noncommittally. "Now, let's look at the pattern of results. First, on the tests that measure your intelligence, memory and so on, you performed well above average. You are obviously a very bright lady, a conclusion which may not surprise you, your family or friends!"

"Well, I don't know but thank you."

"Turning to the personality test, the answers you give to the various questions allow us to classify your character into various categories and then measure, if you will, which of those categories are prominent in your personality and which are not. The human mind is, of course, very complex so this is, in some ways, a rather crude tool but it can be helpful, as I said earlier."

"You do score rather highly - above average, at least - on what are termed demoralisation, aberrant experiences, ideas of persecution and dysfunctional negative emotions but low on antisocial behaviour and hypomanic activation."

"What those strange terms mean is probably, in essence, that you have some low moods, perhaps self-doubt. You may be prone to feelings that are not helpful to you, such as anxiety, persecution or a sensation of vulnerability. Some of your thoughts are unusual, for most people that is. However, you do not show antisocial tendencies - not in the normal sense, at least - and are not prone to impulsive behaviour. We will discuss all this, and more specific things, in more detail in due course but, first off, do you feel that is a fair overall assessment of you?"

Muonasa had never really thought about what sort of a person she was but she agreed because it seemed easier and she respected him.

At the end of an hour of further enquiry, and after Muonasa had left the consulting room, Dr. Haynes leant back in his chair and reflected. She did not score highly on the

"Ideas of Persecution" section of the Minnesota Personality Inventory nor, in interview, did she show any kind of generalised feelings of persecution.   But she did show vulnerability.   Could the whole business of a potentially incurable disease - with frankly little evidence to support it - be simply a manifestation of paranoia?   And would that diagnosis also explain her impression of her brother and his behaviour? And maybe her father as well?

On the walk back to her house, Muonasa thought hard about the things that Dr. Haynes had asked her and what he had managed to drag out from the back of her mind somewhere to the front. How he was able to draw things out that no-one else had ever been able to do - or seemingly had ever wanted to do. How he had managed to make her think in a different way. If only he were there with her all the time, maybe he could cure her just by talking. But then, she saw the face of the Nigerian man again and remembered the spirit.

Chapter 4

This was a new morning and a new day to come. Muonasa reached for her stone but she knew that at any time Adedayo could appear at the door with his latest requisition. She gazed into the stone but all she could see was a smooth beige surface, decorated around the edge with motifs of heads in red and black. She closed her eyes but no image appeared. Maybe later, she decided. She put the stone back in its position next to the lamp on her bedside table.

She had as much wash as she could manage with her limited facilities, decided she needed some food if she was to have another day like the one before and, after dressing, went down to the kitchen.

She hurried down the fracturing wooden stairs. About halfway down, she could hear the sound of a kettle about to boil and something moving about in the kitchen. The light was on and the shadows of this as yet mysterious entity were cascading across the corridor wall as in a dance macabre. The image served only to confound in Muonasa's mind the dark, unsettling nature of the world into which she had arrived, travelling there in good faith with wholesome intentions, only to find that, so far at least, a dense cloud had obliterated her bright visions. But the stone had given her hope, hope just to carry on to a shining horizon on the edge of her quagmire.

As she rounded the near jamb of the doorway, the oppressions that dominated her mind were temporarily freed when she discovered a natural and welcome explanation for her fears: another female human being, going about the normal activities of the morning: making breakfast. In fact, at that point, it was she who was more alarmed than Muonasa.

"Oh, you made me jump!" she said, just avoiding major scalds from her cup of hot coffee that was now shaking in her hand.

"I am very sorry," said Muonasa.

The girl was black, obviously African. She was wearing a short, black leather skirt, black tights, a bright red and yellow chiffon blouse and black, patent leather slingback shoes. Her hair was black, shining, long and wavy but swept back against her temples and tied in a bun. The light sent reflective sparkles from the glitter on her cheeks. Her mouth was accentuated by bright red lipstick.

"Well, hello!" said the girl, now laughing. "Since you came down the stairs rather than up them, I guess you are the new arrival."

"Yes, I guess so," said Muonasa.

"Settled in? Enjoying your new job? Sorry, I shouldn't be so flippant but this place stinks and you have to do something to stop yourself going insane."

"I am Muonasa."

"Yes, hello Muonasa; I am Adebanke. Pleased to meet you, if it doesn't sound like an insult, welcoming you into this hell-hole. Which part of Nigeria are you from?"

"How do you know I am from Nigeria?" asked Muonasa.

Adebanke diverted her gaze and stared fixedly towards the wall. She spoke rapidly and passionately, as if trying to incite a crowd. "Because everyone who passes through here is from Nigeria. They've got it organised to a T. Promise of a new life, guaranteed work, sponsorship for the travel and all the other necessary bits and pieces, organised accommodation. They sound like a high class tour operator, don't they? And basically, that's what they are. Except what they don't tell you is that if you don't sleep with every man who walks through the door - and do everything that is conjured up in these weirdos' minds in the way of sexual deviation, then you will be out the door without a penny and living rough - or possibly worse. So far, I haven't had the courage to find out exactly what would happen."

She turned towards Muonasa, who was looking at the floor, head slightly bowed.

"Sorry, Muonasa," said Adebanke. "I shouldn't stoke up your no doubt pretty bad feelings, especially since you have only just got here and haven't yet got over the shock. If indeed it really has hit you yet - sorry, that's not very helpful either. Well, anyway, I am from Iba."

"Not far from me," said Muonasa. "I am from Iree."

"How long have you been here?" asked Muonasa.

"Eight months. That's a hell of a lot of men. But they all love me, they say - yeah, right!"

"Are they all different? No, I mean do the same men come back or does each come only once?"

"Well, they mostly only come once with each visit!" And she laughed out loud. "Sorry again, I'll try to be serious. No, they mostly return. They might at first do a round of the girls on offer but then tend to focus on their favourite. And then you are stuck with them. To be honest, though, I think that's better because at least you get to know them. And to be fair, some are quite kind and the others - well, at least you eventually get used to their nasty ways so it doesn't come as a shock anymore. You arrived about three days ago or so, didn't you?"

"Yes."

"So have you been initiated?"

"Yes, yesterday. There were four - or possibly five. I can't remember."

"Or don't want to. Be calm, Muonasa. We must talk some more but soon I am going to have to get ready for today's onslaught. Don't you worry for today - he will give you the day off so you can adjust."

"All heart!"

"Wouldn't that be nice? Sadly, the real reason is that he cannot do with girls getting hysterical, kicking up a fuss and generally having a bad influence on the other whores and the smooth running of his nasty business." She gave Muonasa a quick hug and left with her bowl of porridge. "See you later!"

Muonasa returned to her room. She lay on her bed, relishing the moments of calm provided to her by the comforting words of her possibly only friend in this desert of love; at least today she would not have to endure what she did yesterday. But tomorrow? How could she go through it all again, that vile abuse of everything she had ever held dear? But she had been told by that man in Nigeria that it was all necessary to make her better and she must go through with it. If so, then she would. But could she?

She slept for a while, not sure how long because she had not been provided with a clock - *Was that deliberate?* she asked herself. When she awoke, she was hungry; she realised that the feelings generated by the interaction with Adebanke had temporarily suppressed her appetite and she had forgotten to eat. After hastily gobbling down some pieces of bread and jam from the kitchen, she went back to her room and again lay on her bed.

Her eyes scanned aimlessly across the ceiling. In the browned cracks of the plaster, she built images, at first simple shapes, such as squares and triangles but, as her focus deepened, she perceived letters, objects and even faces. Sometimes the pictures seemed to move against each other so that she envisaged and developed a whole story line around the characters that developed. Soon she was lost in a world of fantasy; the visions even seemed to acquire colour.

Her time of personal escape was interrupted by a knock on the door, which opened without waiting for a response from within. It was Adedayo.

"I've brought you some new clothes," he said dispassionately. "I thought the image would suit you."

On the bed, he laid some powder blue hot pants, a short-sleeved, peacock, crew-neck T-shirt, white satin ballet pumps, a white cotton strapless bra and three pairs of white silk and lace panties. "Keep them clean," he said; "you have plenty of water," and moved towards the door. "Oh, and your hair - deal with it." Muonasa, whose hair was styled in ringlets, was told to let it flow freely around her shoulders "in a gesture of innocence." Turning briefly before he left, he said, "Be ready for tomorrow."

She paced slowly around the room for a minute or two and stopped by the wardrobe. Tilting her head as if to study its surface, she ran her fingers up and down the oak upright on its right and scraped off some of the flaking varnish with the fingernails of her right hand. After rubbing the fragments between her thumb and fingers, she watched the debris as it fell like dark brown snowflakes to the floor; a moment of art in a philistine world.

Muonasa went to the window and looked out again at her new world, as she had a number of times since arrival at the house. On one of her previous visual trips to the outside world, she had cleared a patch in the grimy window, using a pair of socks that she had then thrown away in disgust. She re-examined her environment through her newly created and only functional window. Sadly, but not surprisingly, it had changed little but she relished in the small differences: the hobbling man was replaced by someone of similar appearance lying in the gutter at the end of the road, empty bottle in his hand. *How long has he been there?* she thought. *I don't remember seeing him last time I looked.* She transferred her gaze when he moved and she was satisfied that he was not dead; *well, not yet anyway.* The dirty old syringe and needle were still there but she could just make out that they had gained companions of similar appearance but much younger. The concrete wall and factory unit were unchanged except that the black BMW was not there; but then she had noticed that it had come and gone over the last day or two. *Why is he coming and going in a posh car to and from an empty factory?* she thought. *Where does he get the money for that car?*

She looked back to the left, where she saw a man of about thirty, standing close to the street corner but sheltered and partially hidden between some old stone pillars that she guessed once formed part of a grand entrance to some mansion of bygone days. He was shuffling nervously from one foot to the other, occasionally peeking out from between the pillars to look down the road to left and right. His hands were plunged deep into the pockets of a rather oversized hoodie. His lower half was bedecked by faded, baggy jeans but bright white trainers, obviously new. Even from where she stood,

Muonasa could see that he had a fine stubble on his chin but his head was bald.

After a few minutes, another younger man appeared around the corner, to the first man's right. In contrast to the first man, who looked to be slightly overweight, the other was thin, almost emaciated. He was dressed in a shabby, dirty white or grey T-shirt, grey tracksuit bottoms and worn trainers. He moved slowly with a slight stoop. When he came level with the man in the hoodie, he turned slightly to the left to greet him, stopped suddenly and momentarily overbalanced, regaining his stability on one foot. A few words were spoken, obviously softly as judged by their gestures; the thin man handed over some rolled up banknotes; the other reached into his pocket and placed something into the palm of the other; Muonasa could see not what. Nothing else was said; the thin man shuffled off; the other walked in the direction of the black BMW, which Muonasa noticed was now occupied by a large man in a smart, black jacket, sitting in the driver's seat.

She ambled back towards the centre of the room and sat on the bed when her left hand happened to alight on the T-shirt brought in by Adedayo. She picked it up in the one hand and stared at it with an air of unfamiliarity, almost lack of recognition of what she was holding. Placing it back down, she picked up each of the other garments in turn and studied them with the same expression. With the hot pants, she looked automatically into the inside of the waistband to check that they were the right size. When her exploration through her new wardrobe reached the underwear, she sighed and put it back down.

Muonasa reached for her stone and, holding it cradled on the palmar surfaces of the interlocked fingers of her two hands, looked down at it. As usual, her concentration became fixed on the area within the decorated boundary. She closed her eyes and let her mind wander. The male voice appeared again and told her to continue to think positively because she had luck on her side although it may not appear so just now. She should regard the new clothes as a welcome gift and he had no doubt that she would look very pretty in them. Everything else was just a job; like all jobs, there were downsides but there were also good moments. So, he said, she should press on and see it all through; it would be worth it in the end.

She opened her eyes and, returning the stone to its usual place, lay down on the bed. Soon drowsiness began to overtake her; she fell asleep and began to dream.

In the depths of her mind, she found herself in her parents' first home in Nigeria, a young child, seated on her mother's knee. It was evening; she was in pyjamas, obviously ready for bed. She looked up into her mother's eyes.

"Tell me a story," said Muonasa.

"Well, just a quick one," said her mother, *"because you really ought to be in bed now. Otherwise you will be tired in the morning and won't want to play. And that would be a shame because you will miss all the fun with your friends."*

"All right," said Muonasa.

"Well," began her mother, *"once there was a boy, whose mother had sadly died when he was a baby so he lived with his father, a chief. The father was very good at hunting with a bow and arrow and taught his son to do the same. The boy practised*

and practised, at first hunting birds and lizards until he was very good."

"When he was about ten years old, he took over from his father as chief. He was in charge of all the slaves but they did not like him and planned to get rid of him so he ran away into the forest. Because he was now a good hunter, he did not come to any harm and managed to find enough food to eat."

"One day, he bent down to take a drink of water from a lake but he heard a voice telling him not to drink. Not knowing where it came from, he thought he had better take notice so he went to find some somewhere else."

"The next day, he met an old woman in the forest. She told him that it was she who had called out to him at the lake because there was a bad juju spirit in the lake who wanted to do the boy harm so she had protected him. She then took him to a stream from which she removed a bright stone and gave it to the boy."

"She told him to go to a particular place in the forest and dig into the ground, where he would find a lot of buried money. He must then use the money to build a house with many rooms. Into one of the rooms, he should place the stone that she had given to him. Whenever he wanted anything, he just had to go into that room, tell the stone and his wishes would be granted."

"So the boy did as he was told: he built the house and put the stone into one of the rooms. Whenever he wanted anything, he went into that room and told the stone and someone would magically bring the things to him. As a result, he grew very rich and powerful and ruled a large town. Everyone was happy to work with him again. How grateful he was to that magic stone!"

As her mother finished speaking, she glanced down at her child, just to see her eyes close, her breathing deepen and her limbs relax. She carried the sleeping child to her bedroom, laid her in her bed and closed the door enough to leave a small gap so she could hear if her daughter was distressed in the night.

Muonasa awoke and opened her eyes but was surprised not to see the familiar comforts of her childhood bedroom but an adult bed, strewn with new clothes, in a room with a wardrobe with flaking varnish, a small bedside table and a grimy window. Muonasa had returned to reality.

Swinging her legs over the side of the bed, she sat with her face in her hands for a minute or two as her consciousness fully returned before sitting up straight and reaching out with her right hand to pick up the stone. She turned her head to the right and gave it a pensive but brief look before returning it to its place. Pondering what to do next, she was alerted by a strange sound from somewhere outside her room. As was now usual, any unexpected event precipitated in her a wave of anxiety.

She went over to the door to her room, turned the weathered brass knob slowly and gently opened the door a few inches, just enough so that she could gaze through the gap without being seen herself. A slight squeak from the rusty door hinge caused her heart to skip a beat and draw backwards but she settled quickly when she realised no-one had heard. She resumed her position of vigilance. In one of the rooms below, maybe even the one next to Adebanke, she just heard the sound of someone sobbing.

Then, she heard the noise of footsteps on the wooden staircase; simultaneously, the sobbing ceased; the ensuing silence seemed to transmit a wave of emotion from the room below that conveyed recognition, expectation - and fear. Muonasa knew that the girl in the room - the pitch of the sobbing could be produced only by a female - had heard those footsteps many times before and awaited their sequel with horrifying familiarity.

Adebanke was working that day but Muonasa vowed that, at the first opportunity, she would speak with her again. Despite their only brief encounter, she felt that her new acquaintance had already assumed a reference point for normality in a situation that was otherwise devoid of it. Indeed, Adebanke may be her only friend - apart, that is, from Dr. Haynes.

Muonasa's next day of work was in essence a repetition of her first. And so was the next. And the next. Some of the men were kind; others were verging on deranged. The one consideration that Adedayo had shown her was to tell her emphatically that she must call out to him if she felt she were in danger. He explained that some clients were vigorous, and dominating and even liked to engage in a bit of force and that was, of course, acceptable but there must be no risk to her life or long-term health. Considerate, maybe - or perhaps just a safety net to guarantee continuation of his workforce. Muonasa's new clothes seemed to carry appeal, perhaps because Adedayo had carefully selected the men who might appreciate them.

Between clients, Muonasa routinely resorted to the comfort of her stone, which she was in no doubt gave her the support necessary to continue in activities that would otherwise be anathema to her. As a result, she learned to cope with her new life, initially one day at a time but later the daily black moments merged into one continuous grey background that she could almost ignore. But not quite.

She also got to see more of Adebanke because, following a series of good reports from the clients, Adedayo agreed to let them have days off together so they could meet up in one of their bedrooms to chat or go out to walk around the local area. At the next encounter with the stone following Adedayo's pronouncement, the voice reminded Muonasa that she must have the stone with her at all times or he, behind the voice, would not be able to protect her. She must be careful not to forget it whenever she left the house.

"How do you get a good report from someone for lying there and not doing very much?" asked Muonasa once, in one of the lighter moods that meetings with Adebanke sometimes brought.

"That's what they like about you," replied her friend. "It goes with your fancy dress!"

"Well, I'm not sure about that," said Muonasa. "Some of them don't behave as if they like me very much."

"Oh, tell me about it!" said Adebanke. "Some of the guys that our friendly pimp has chosen for me are complete bastards. If you judged all men by this lot, you'd be either celibate or lesbian! But then, the type who come to a whore house, especially one like this, are either so feeble that they cannot get it anywhere else or have such a perverted idea of the opposite sex that they think this kind of thing is normal."

"I guess so," said Muonasa. "I try to switch my mind off to somewhere else when I am with the men or at least make a conscious effort to come back to normal between them. But it's hard."

"Well, I wish I could," said her friend.

"What makes Adedayo do this?" said Muonasa.

"Well, I wonder if it could be money," replied Adebanke. "Sorry, I keep forgetting that you are new to the game and I shouldn't jest. Yes, money and more money. He's got to do something to feed his habit."

"Drugs?"

"Now you are learning! Yes, drugs - and alcohol."

"And the girls - what do they all do to get away from it all?"

"Sadly, most of them follow Adedayo's example. It's the easy way of escape - except it isn't. The money they get from Adedayo goes on drugs so they are out of it when not working and sometimes when they are. But that's great for Adedayo and the big guys because they are kept under control. That's why you never see the other girls, working or out of it - that's their life. But I for one am determined not to go down that road. I have too much self-respect although none of the pervos that come here would know it."

"So sometimes he will be so drugged up that he wouldn't be able to respond if we were in trouble?"

"Oh, he would! Unlike some, and most of the girls, he functions pretty well on the stuff. Well, most of the time, anyway. And, although I hate him, he doesn't treat us badly - well, not him personally - though I hate the garbage that he brings through my bedroom door. Amazingly, some of the girls have got a real soft spot for him."

"All I have seen are signs of horrible degradation. There have been all sorts of nasty looking people coming up the stairs - not all, I admit, and so far I've been spared - but I've heard girls crying, really crying."

"All that is true, Muonasa, but you won't hear the ones that have settled in because they are just getting on with it. And those are the ones who are high on drugs as well. It's another method of payment - but they have to earn it so, in their own twisted way of thinking, they work hard to get their returns.   Which therefore means that they are in favour, treated well, get what they want, get to like the people who provide it; it's a big vicious circle."

"And what's in it for them in the long run?"

"Not much.   More of the same until the drugs or some maniac takes them off the face of the earth; then they are forgotten, not least because there is nobody else around who cares and there is always some other poor loser ready to walk into their shoes. So everybody is happy."

On one of their times together, it was decided that Adebanke would give Muonasa a guided tour of the local area. They turned left out of the house, went to the end of the road, where Muonasa had seen the exchange between the thin man and the man in the hoodie, and turned right. Until then, apart from visits to church and her doctor, this was the furthest that Muonasa had ventured from the house, her visions from her bedroom window instilling fear as to what or whom she might come across that was worse than she had experienced already.

"Don't worry," reassured her friend.   "The alkies, smackheads and pushers usually keep themselves to themselves and the big guys keep a low profile - for pretty obvious reasons."

"What, to keep out of the eyes of the police?"

"Too right!" said Adebanke. "If the cops do a swoop on the area, which they do from time to time - I guess so that they can convince people that they are doing something to clean up the area, which they are not - Mister Big Fish will make sure that it's the small fry who end up on the end of the line and not him."

Adebanke led Muonasa about half a mile down the road before turning left at a T-junction into an area of small shops and cafes and beckoned her friend to follow her into a small coffee house with four or five tables.

"I like this place," she said, "not least because of the charming man behind the bar!" The middle-aged Egyptian smiled back at her in recognition.

"Will your friend also have coffee?" he asked. Following a nod from Muonasa, he set to preparing the drinks and the girls settled at one of the tables. Over the next forty minutes or so, they exchanged their personal histories, in particular how they had come to end up in a life of prostitution when neither of them had any intention of doing so when they left Nigeria.

Adebanke explained that she came from quite a poor family who, wanting the best for her, had urged her to come to England to get training for a good job that was not available to someone like her back home. They even thought that she might be able to go to university because she seemed to be quite bright at school. From word of mouth, they had discovered an agency that would sponsor young girls to do just that. They would find a placement in England and pay for the travel and the first six months' accommodation and living expenses. In return, they took twenty percent of the girl's first year's earnings, provided she was in a stable job for at least two years and earning more than a certain amount.

"It didn't seem as if I could lose," she said. "Yes, I'd be away from my family but the agency also said that they would aid with resettling in Nigeria in a good job that would use all the training I had received in England when the time seemed right - which was usually a few years later at most. Naturally, I could stay in England if I wanted to and if the country would have me. So we leapt at it! Better than cleaning floors in the local school!"

"Except it was all crap," she added, with an air of resignation. "I'm earning money, all right, and I get to keep some so I can live but there are people here and back in Nigeria who are getting a lot more out of me than I am."

"How do they get away with it? The authorities must know about it; why don't they clamp down?"

"Because money talks, I guess."

"Have you told your family what happened? What was their reaction?"

Adebanke took on one of her rare expressions of anguish. "No, I daren't," she said. "It's been made pretty clear what would happen if I did."

"Like what?"

"Well, it would be the end of me - literally - and possibly my family too. In fact, now I think about it, that's probably why they have encouraged me to talk to you - because they knew that I would warn you of your own fate if you talked to anyone or tried to get away. It would be easier to let me do their dirty work for them."

A few tears fell onto Muonasa's cheeks. She put her arm around her friend's shoulders, partly in sympathy for her but partly in a gesture of mutual solidarity. After a few minutes' silence, she asked:

"How do they know that I wouldn't have done something already?"

"If you notice, there is no access to a phone in the house; you are not allowed a mobile phone; all post has to be sent through Adedayo. They know you have not gone far outside on your own and they will have been watching you. They could afford to bide their time until you were pretty much entrenched."

"Is this all Adedayo's doing?"

"Oh, no! He's just the drug-fuelled minion. The big guys are clear-headed, ruthless and somewhere else."

The two fell silent again, each lost in their own, albeit similar, thoughts: a shift from the self-nurtured sense of resignation to a deep misgiving concerning their long-term fate; a move from the uncertainty about when their current fortunes would change to a profound fear that they may never; a kindling of an awareness that the future may not bring relief but even something worse; that their hopes may be terminated not by release but by a premature end to life in any form.

"Let's go for a walk!" said Adebanke, suddenly breaking the silence and rising abruptly from her seat. Muonasa followed. Once outdoors, conversation about trivia allowed them both to resume the artificial feelings of normality that had sustained them before the evils of their real world had encroached upon their peace.

About half a mile down the road, they approached an old church in Gothic design, surrounded on three sides by a graveyard. Adebanke led the way through a small wrought iron gate on to a path that crossed in front of the church, diagonally between the gravestones. Muonasa urged her companion to stop for a while so she could enjoy the architecture and then led her among the gravestones, reading the epitaphs.

"Look at this, Adebanke," she said with passion. "How tragic is that? A woman and two children, obviously all from the same family, died within two years of each other. And over here, three children, all under five, died in the same year, seventeen eighty-four. What causes that?"

"Maybe the kids caught something from each other," said Adebanke. "And the woman - maybe she killed the two kids and then herself."

Muonasa laughed. "You've got a vivid imagination!" Then, turning pensive, added: "But you might be right about the three children."

They wandered together for several minutes before Muonasa said: "I like graveyards."

"Why? Everybody's dead!"

"Yes, exactly, but each one of these people has a story to tell - if they could. The woman and the two children - what life did they have? What horrors did the other mother feel when three of her children, maybe all the children she had, died virtually all at once? Sadly, we will never know. And there's the fascination - because all we can do is speculate. Somewhere that woman is waiting to tell us her story and no doubt will when we meet her again."

"Do you believe in all that stuff - afterlife, heaven and the rest?"

"Yes, don't you?"

"Well, I was brought up as a Christian but I find it hard now."

"So do I sometimes but I have no doubt that God will make everything right in the end, through the mediation of his son, Jesus Christ."

"You're beginning to sound like a priest!"

"Sorry, maybe I am. But I do hold that faith close to my heart. It's the only thing that gives me the strength to carry on."

"Are you going to church here in London? Don't worry about that; the powers that are controlling us won't be worried about it; they will see you as a harmless nonentity! But seriously, I admire you - good for you! I honestly hope your faith will bring you everything you wish for. Really, I mean it!"

"Thank you," said Muonasa. "Yes, I have found a church. It's the same one that my psychiatrist, Mark Haynes, attends."

"Is it the church or the man that draws you in?" said Adebanke, as a cheeky grin spread across her face.

"Well, maybe both," was the reply.

"Whoa!" said Adebanke, laughing out loud.

They ambled over to some newer stones on the edge of the graveyard. "Now here," said Muonasa, "you've got a dedication from a brother to a dear sister and thanks for her life and the joy she gave and then, three years later, he was lying next to her. Doesn't that get to you? But the good news is that they are now together in heaven."

"Do you have brothers or sisters?" asked Adebanke.

"I have a brother. He's here in London, as a matter of fact, although I haven't met up with him yet."

"Oh wow!" said her friend. "That's great! You are so lucky. I am sure you'll be able to get to see him soon. I expect you can't wait."

"I'm not sure," said Muonasa. "He doesn't think much of me, never has, but especially recently. If he knew what I was doing he'd have a fit. I sometimes think he'd rather I'd never existed. He's much more religious - rigidly so - than I am. In fact, he's a fanatic. Oh well, let's move on," she said and started walking.

They walked along the yew hedge around the edge of the graveyard back to the path and followed it for a few yards to another gate that opened on to a side road leading down to a busy main road. As they walked alongside the streaming traffic towards the West, Muonasa could see a number of tall buildings clustered together, the setting afternoon sun casting a golden halo around their borders. In a strange way, the random traffic noise and the shimmering rays combined to produce a son-et-lumière effect in Muonasa's mind. *How lovely*, she thought.

"This is the hotel district," said Adebanke. "I guess that you have not had the honour of a visit there yet."

"What do you mean?"

"Well, Adedayo has some regular clients who stay there on business and, of course, all needs must be met. So, when you are fully trained up, as it were, he will probably get you to ply your trade over there. That is, once he trusts you or, to be more specific, when the powers that be trust you and he gets told what to do. It's much the same as back at our place although they might be a bit nicer - well, they are certainly better off so, if you are lucky, you might get a glass of wine. It partly depends on how much of a hurry they are in!" She laughed again. "No, but really, you are mostly asked to spend the night there so it's a bit better - as long as you leave early in the morning so no-one will discover their dirty secret. But you can never quite tell; if they do turn nasty, Adedayo won't be there to look after you. I've been lucky so far."

"I don't know whether I should look forward to that or not."

"I wouldn't look forward to much in this life if I were you; then you won't be disappointed. Each day, I'd just thank God that you are still alive. Let's go and have a drink."

Chapter 5

Muonasa continued to see Mark Haynes at regular intervals. From his perspective, it was probably more often than was necessary but the more he probed the deeper reaches of her character, the more fascinating it became. To the lay person, it was probably mundane but to someone like him, who specialised in the working of the mind, it was more interesting than any book or movie.

It was becoming clear, to him at least, that her belief that she had a serious disease was false but that did not mean that she did not need help, especially since the belief was so profound. Furthermore, where did this idea of a serious disease come from? Yes, she had said that the information stemmed from a traditional rural doctor in Nigeria but on what basis? Dr. Haynes was no expert on medical practice that did not conform to western traditions and he realised that some foreign treatments, such as acupuncture, had gained acceptance in the West. Nevertheless, it seemed likely to him that the Nigerian doctor was practising folklore medicine at best. *I may be biased,* he thought, *but my guess is that the fellow is frankly wrong.*

But he realised that the story did not stop there. Why was Muonasa so convinced of the veracity of this diagnosis that she had followed the Nigerian doctor's advice and travelled to the UK for treatment? And why, despite many consultations he had now had with her, in which he had tried to draw her round to the notion that things were not as bad as they seemed, had she stuck rigidly to her belief?

The only realistic possibility he was moving towards was that the belief is a delusion. "*A fixed, false belief held with strong conviction despite overwhelming evidence to the contrary,*" he recited to himself, like a medical student in revision. But Dr. Haynes also reflected that this delusion, if that is what it is, occurred in isolation, in the absence of any other stigmata of mental illness. It was true that she had vulnerability, some paranoia and some low moods but not, in themselves, sufficient to warrant a psychiatric diagnosis. Could this Nigerian doctor have somehow implanted this delusion in her mind, he wondered, but immediately dismissed it as fanciful nonsense. *Now we're entering the realms of mind control*, he thought, *and we know that does not exist.*

And then it dawned: supposing this Nigerian doctor does not exist and his creation is a figment of the girl's imagination? And further, if she does believe he exists and she also believes that this imaginary person has given her instructions that she feels duty bound to follow, even to another country, how much worse a delusion is that? If she is so deluded, he thought, she must have features of some more general psychiatric disorder - but she does not. At least, he has not found any so far. Next consultation, he must make more detailed enquiries to see if she has a psychotic disorder; does she, for example, have any disorder of thinking or suffer hallucinations, seeing or hearing things that do not exist, that might indicate a diagnosis of schizophrenia? He was beginning to feel more confident that she might, after all, fall within the more normal domain of psychiatric practice and that he might therefore be able to help her from well within his experience without having to stretch his mental analytical skills too far into the unknown.

For Muonasa, the consultations were not as often as she would have liked. The medical input to her condition was adequate, she guessed, but there was more than that. Even professional relationships, she told herself, have a human side as well as a practical one. And she was benefitting from both aspects in her involvement with Dr. Haynes. He was working on her disease - and she acknowledged that was the primary reason for consulting him - but there was no doubt that she also felt better in herself from a human interaction with him. Indeed, as far as her sense of wellbeing was concerned, she was not sure which aspect was providing the greater boost. Did it really matter? All she knew was that she enjoyed being with him.

"Hello, Becky; hello Mark. Do come in!" The hostess in her long white gown did a mini-pirouette on one foot, vacating a space between her and the open, heavy, oak front door. Her guests passed through; she leant forward to give weight to the door as she closed it and followed Dr. and Mrs. Haynes into the orangery.

The room was big enough to show the pink marble tiles between the feet of the twenty to thirty guests. The six-foot neo-Grecian urns lining each of the long walls were of such quality that most observers believed they stemmed from antiquity. Evening light from the four almost floor-to-ceiling arched windows to the right cast a tangential glow onto the people closest its source, creating a silhouette effect that made them look abstract and mysterious, removed from real life. The others looked dull, colourless and uninspiring by comparison.

Eight girls in white, A-line, satin dresses extending only to mid-thigh, and wearing matching chokers, floated amongst the crowd. They carried silver trays bearing Georgian flutes filled with vintage Veuve Clicquot champagne. Two of them approached the Haynes as they descended the flight of three shallow stairs into the body of the room, one from each side. Dr. and Mrs. Haynes each took a glass of wine. Mozart's 21st piano concerto was playing through the Bang and Olufsen speakers, one in each corner of the room.

"My goodness! This is the theme music from the film 'Last Year at Marienbad'," said Mark to Becky.

"I recognise it," she replied. "We saw it together at a specialist picture house in Soho. I remember it well because a storm was blowing outside; the simple building was shaking; the lights were flickering. It seemed as if it portended the end of the world - or life as we know it."

"That seems a bit dramatic!" said Mark

"Well, it's often the unwary who are most vulnerable to the unexpected," said a voice to the right and just behind them.

They turned to see a short, thin lady, in her mid-forties, dressed in an ethnic, floor-length, brightly and multicoloured cotton dress, with an elfin face and dark brown hair.

"Sorry," she said, still with an appealing smile. "I couldn't help but overhear."

After introductions, a series of pleasantries, and conversation about the murals, Mark felt bold enough to return to their opening verbal exchange.

"So how do you think we should prepare for the unexpected, Theresa, when, by definition, the unexpected is not predicted? You may have been joking, of course, but, it's an interesting philosophical question. Or maybe it isn't! Tell me if I am being boring."

"No, not at all. I do find these kinds of things of great interest. I just bear in mind that one thing leads to another. Do something and something else will follow as a consequence. A storm might cause a building to shake but then a shaking building might cause the street to shake and ultimately the whole country, continent and world will shake. If not resolved, the shaking will cause the earth to fragment. Hence the end of life as we know it. So, if you can tap into something earlier in the chain, you can see what it is likely to bring about. In other words, predict the unexpected. "

"Well, that's logical, Theresa, but how likely is that sequence of events to happen? Even if you spotted something earlier on, how would you know what it was likely to cause? Because a building is shaking does not mean that the street will necessarily shake or that that will cause the earth to shake."

Theresa continued: "You cannot apply statistics to the unknown. To get an answer, you need a contact with the unknown - unknown to mankind in general, that is."

"And who is that contact?"

"I am."

Over in the corner, a teenage girl was ambling about purposelessly on her own. She had agreed to come with her parents under pressure, particularly from her father, but it had not taken long before she realised that the acquiescence had been a mistake. She certainly had no desire to speak to any of the other people at the party although several who knew her and her family had attempted to draw her into conversation. Her standing alone brought out the concerns of her fellow guests and increased the tendency for them to impose their caring nature on her personal space. Thus she had taken to moving around aimlessly, not getting too close to anyone and avoiding eye contact.

Mark had not taken to Theresa's brand of philosophy and had moved over to a group of four old friends where he knew he could start a meaningful discussion about the quality of the wine. Becky half wished she could get away too because she was beginning to feel a little uncomfortable but another half of her wanted to explore what this new acquaintance stood for - or thought she stood for. She and Theresa ambled together through the assembled company, in uncertain conversation. Becky was attentive but hesitant; Theresa was confident but cautious, as if biding her time.

This woman had said, in essence, thought Becky, *that she was a contact with the unknown - unknown to mankind, that is. Was this a figurative reference - an insight into human nature - an ability to understand people in a way that they could not do themselves, a psychoanalyst by any other name? Or was she being literal? That there was a force outside of humankind with which she could communicate? Of course, the latter was not new - mediums, seances, ghost-hunters, poltergeist-spotters, exorcists had long captivated not only the imagination of intelligent people over the centuries but also their actions. Fortunately, the habit of burning people at the stake had become unfashionable for a while.*

Becky gently questioned her new companion.

"No, I am not being figurative," said Theresa, " although human nature and the world beyond interact in a way that few people understand. I am just fortunate in having access to that relationship."

"Do you mean that you are a medium?"

"People know a medium as someone who communicates with the dead. I would not claim anything so specific. I communicate with the spirit world - spirits of live people, spirits of the dead and, yes, unknown spirits probably as well."

"And you believe that you do?"

"I know I do."

Theresa had produced something of a mood change in Becky - or, at least, brief swings of emotion, from elation and involvement to disquiet and disbelief. The medium - let's call her that for short - made no logical sense but her words were somehow intriguing. Her persona was magnetic; her words were adhesive. Her smile was attractive; her eyes were penetrating. Becky stayed close to her side as they wandered aimlessly through the room, shuffling around the other guests without overt acknowledgement of their existence. Soon the mixed emotions that she was experiencing coalesced into one of distrust.

Almost symbolically, the guests to left and right ebbed away as the two moved in a diagonal towards the corner of the room - like the departing processional from church as the newly-weds leave for the photographs and people look happy. At the end of this man-created aisle stood the teenager.

Becky sighed. "Theresa," she said, "I'd like you to meet my daughter, Amy," although, from what she had learned so far of Theresa, the thought of her daughter's getting to know this lady in any way more than superficial instilled in her considerable disquiet. But such was the variable luck implicit in random meetings. "Amy, this is Theresa."

Amy's innate good manners, consistent with indulgence from middle-class parents, precipitated automatically the string of words and bodily gestures to indicate that the new meeting of Theresa was nothing less than a delight. But Theresa was too skilled in her analysis of human behaviour to miss the subtle pointers to a girl with inner turmoil: the intermittent, brief loss of eye contact; the slightly flexed, motionless head; the brief, stroking movements of her thumb on her other fingers. She looked intently into Amy's eyes and Amy responded in kind.

Rebecca was not going to run the risk that her teenage daughter's vulnerable state could be further compromised by someone with - how should she describe it? - *strange ideas*, she thought euphemistically. A fascinating person, yes, for someone like Becky who prided herself on being reasonably stable - well, most of the time - and who could switch off the conversation or the relationship if she found them uncomfortable. But Amy was different, or at least had become so over the last year or so. Rebecca had always thought that her daughter had inherited a large proportion of her genes from her so she could be confident that she understood the workings of Amy's mind. But recently things had changed: the subtle mood swings, the verbal discourse which, on first hearing, sounded normal but which displayed fundamental flaws in logic on closer analysis; the mild paranoia; the sudden shock-like movements of her body as if something invisible had momentarily alarmed her.

Mark Haynes had once told his wife that doctors fall into two categories as far as their families are concerned: those who apply their expertise with anxious enthusiasm to every symptom stemming from their spouse and children; and those who seem incapable of acknowledging that home is not a safe haven as far as illness is concerned, that the medical matters of real life cannot be left in the workplace, never to encroach upon the doctor's personal life. He acknowledged that he fell into the latter group. Not only was he unable to make a useful decision when one of his family fell sick - except to consult another doctor - but he also failed to spot the early signs of illness that he would have pounced on in his professional life. Fortunately, his wife had the insight of a good mother and a sufficiently involved relationship with her husband that she could usually tap into his reluctant mind. By these means, Mark had finally acknowledged that his daughter may have changed; he was less certain what to do about it.

Rebecca put her arm around her daughter and guided her away from their new-found companion.

"Lovely to talk to you, Theresa. Do excuse us now; I just want to catch up with someone I have noticed on the other side of the room. She used to have quite a lot of dealings with Amy. Maybe see you later!"

"Who?" asked Amy abruptly. "Who used to have a lot of dealings with me, as you put it?"

"Don't worry now, darling. I just didn't want you to get too involved in conversation with that woman; she's interesting but a bit odd."

Amy glanced back towards Theresa. "I imagine I am capable of making my own assessments."

"I am sure you are."

Rebecca could not hold Amy's attention for long before her daughter wandered off again on her own, surveying abstractedly the paintings, ornaments and other decorations and occasionally picking fragments of food from the buffet table. As she was gazing into the interior of a crystal vase on a table by the French windows, she sensed a presence by her side and slightly behind her. She turned.

"Hello," said Theresa. "You look troubled."

"I am."

"By a spirit?"

"Yes, I think so."

"Here's my card." *Theresa Mayes, Spiritual Counsellor.*

Her father bustled out of his bedroom and, before descending the stairs, shouted into the bedroom to his right, "Amy - are you ready for church?"

"Yes, I think so." Dad was aware of his daughter's recent tendency to sleep in late. His most recent call had followed several at intervals over the previous hour to move her from an inert, slumbering body to an erect, coherent human, dressed reasonably respectably and ready to present herself, not only to God but also to the critical eyes of the local congregation.

Amy adjusted her dress, reached for her hairbrush and looked in the mirror to add the final touches to her image. She was nearly ready and about to go downstairs when she paused at the mirror. Why did she do so, she asked herself, when she knew that a prolonged gaze at her own reflection would bring back her unwanted visitor? And it did, even though all she could see was herself.

Yes, it's me but yet it isn't, she thought. There seemed to be more in the reflection than there was in her, the only possible explanation for which was that something had entered the mirror and merged with her image. When the image was reflected back to her, did that mean that the "something" would also be reflected back and combine with her real body? In order to protect herself, she had to stop looking in the mirror but something kept drawing her back to it. And what about other mirrors? Were they safe? Or could this being move between mirrors, chasing her wherever she went and threatening to enter her body from any place in which she found herself?

Surely, it can't get into church. Go to church - yes, go to church!

"Coming!"

For most people present, the service was lovely. The church choir was in full attendance and later sang its solo, "For Unto Us A Child is Born" in perfect harmony, the sopranos trilling over the basses like nightingales in a dark, sultry Provencal night. Before that, the vicar's sermon on infidelity was incisive and reflective, elaborating and clarifying (if indeed it were necessary) the bible reading, Hebrews, Chapter 13, verse 4: "Marriage should be honoured by all, and the marriage bed kept pure, for God will judge the adulterer and all the sexually immoral." For nearly an hour in the service, including the sermon, Amy had felt safe.

Muonasa had arrived deliberately five minutes late so she could take a seat near the back without being noticed by the others. She had found the church easily with the aid of the clear instructions from Mark Haynes' secretary, who fortunately had not seemed too bothered by Muonasa's enquiries concerning his favoured place of worship. Muonasa had no clear reason in her mind why she wanted to attend the same service as him but felt that she would gain spiritually by involving herself in his activities and maybe thereby she could absorb something from him that she knew could only make her more comfortable. Already, she felt better just seeing him standing in one of the front pews.

Not long after the sermon, Amy, distracted perhaps by her lack of appreciation of the Handel oratorio, had turned round to scan the church interior. Her gaze settled on Muonasa, who happened to be looking in her direction so their eyes met. Amy did not know why but there seemed, to her, to be some contact between them: for Amy, a sense of familiarity, a focus for some as yet undefined motive of whatever nature, a slight sense of insecurity; for Muonasa, mild anxiety as to why some teenager should be focussing her gaze with more than the normally expected intensity. With the shift from the music to the prayers, Amy turned her head back towards the altar and let her mind sink into a distant world, prompted partly by the holy entreatments of the vicar and partly by her own desire to escape. But the image of Muonasa did not pass.

The congregation departed in smiles and moved to the church hall for coffee and fellowship. Dr. and Mrs. Haynes and their daughter Amy went over to join the others. As Mark reached the back of the church, he noticed Muonasa.

"Muonasa, how lovely to see you here! What a coincidence! I don't think we have seen you here before; what led you to this church, in particular?"

Muonasa explained that she had asked someone for the name of a church that they would recommend and they had suggested this one. She did not elaborate on the details. The commonplace explanation offered by Muonasa seemed to satisfy Mark, whose enquiry had in truth been only a polite, social question, not demanding much in the way of an answer. The two continued in social chit-chat, both deliberately avoiding any reference to their professional relationship.

Amy's mother took no interest in this coming together of acquaintances because she was used to her husband bumping into people with whom he had worked and generally they were not very interesting. Amy, however, seemed more than casually interested and at intervals stared intently albeit briefly towards Muonasa and her father. Her anxiety level began to escalate, despite her repeated attempts to quell it, so she moved away to where her vision of the couple was blocked.

Rebecca took a cup of coffee from the serving hatch and moved towards her daughter, who was now sitting on one of the hard-backed chairs lining one wall and was staring at the floor.

"How are you feeling now, Amy?" she said gently.

"Much the same."

"Are you still having those silly thoughts?"

"They're not silly and they're not even thoughts - he's real," said Amy, trembling slightly.

Her mother sighed. "How do you know he's real?" She then suddenly straightened up from the bent posture she had adopted to speak closely to Amy and continued brusquely: "I can't believe I asked that! Amy - you tell me that you sense something - no, somebody, you are quite clear about that - but you cannot see them; you cannot hear them and you cannot speak to them. Is that right?"

"No. I can speak to them. To it."

"And do they, does it, reply?"

"Not by voice."

"Then by what exactly?"

"By their being."

Her mother softened. "Can we talk about this at home, with your father?"

"We already have."

"Yes, I know, but this time we'll listen; I promise."

"If you wish."

Mrs. Haynes realised that she had reached an impasse in their discussion, particularly in that setting. Fortunately, she was rescued from any decision as to what to do next by the voice of an elderly lady:

"Coffee, Amy?"

"I'll get an orange juice."

Mark and Rebecca Haynes settled down with their daughter Amy in the sitting room of their Georgian townhouse. As his wife and daughter sat down on adjacent chairs, he opened the fuel burner and added another log, using slow, stilted movements that looked as if he was deliberately playing for time. His expression was set; he was obviously deep in thought.

He turned and sat down at one end of a settee, next to his wife on the far side from Amy. His wife sat stiffly, upright with her hands in her lap. He bent forward at the waist to look around his wife into Amy's face. She, however, was looking at the floor.

Unlike previous occasions, when this subject was discussed, her parents managed this time to listen to their daughter's concerns without losing patience. This was not too difficult for her father because he had chosen to be involved peripherally before so most of the story was new to him. He had also always been less inquisitive and patient and more dismissive than his wife, at least as far as Amy was concerned. As Rebecca knew, he was that kind of doctor when dealing with his family.

The questions were largely posed by her mother whilst her father sat listening, at least at first. Amy answered them firmly and concisely, using much the same responses that she had made on all the previous occasions that her mother had asked those questions.

Dr. Haynes had finally decided to take his daughter's problems seriously. "Amy," he said after several minutes, "this being that you sense, that responds to you although not in a form that you can see or hear - is it human?"

Amy usually responded better on the occasions that her father showed a genuine interest. "I don't know," said Amy, still staring at the floor, "but I don't think so."

"Does it threaten you?"

"Well, not directly - it doesn't tell me that something specific is going to happen - but it frightens me."

"And do you think it intends to do that?"

"Yes, definitely."

Mark Haynes went quiet for a few minutes. His wife knew him well enough to understand that this pattern of behaviour - the silence, followed by carefully worded gentle questioning and then more silence - would culminate in a plan. This was the side of him that she admired and so much better than the cursory dismissal of concerns, which was his favoured *modus operandi.* It was best to keep quiet until he spoke. And then he did.

"Amy, I know that you have seen, sorry, experienced this being and I respect that. Sometimes, though, things like that can be due to a weird working of the mind not one that you would be aware of, and that's the point - because, for you, you would not be able to tell whether it was real or a product of the mind."

"I realise that you have no doubt that it is real but the workings of the mind can create the same feeling. I am not doubting you - I am simply asking you to explore what you are feeling from all angles. With that in mind, I wonder if you would agree to see someone who has talents in the psychological as well as the spiritual world."

"I know someone who can do that," he continued. "She would approach your experiences from both angles and, either way, lead you to a path that allows you to come to terms with them."

"Would this person be able to persuade him to leave me?"

"Very likely."

"Who is this?" said his wife, shocked by her husband's pronouncement, quite a contrast to his usual type of planning. She asked with an expression that combined bemusement with cynicism, wide-eyed, staring into his face with a twisted smile.

"A lecturer in the Psychology Department. Her expertise is cognitive behavioural therapy, which is a treatment now well recognised to be successful in correcting, shall we say, faulty thinking. However, she also believes in the spiritual world and, believe it or not, claims to have some communication with it."

"Is she mad?" said his wife, with a slight sneer, thinking briefly of the encounter with the woman at the party.

"No," said Mark firmly. "Definitely not."

"Are you able to judge, may I ask? Remember, you are a consultant in psychiatry, not, dare I suggest it as relevant, theology."

"Are you willing to see her?" he asked, ignoring his wife.

"Yes," said Amy, without moving. But thoughts of Theresa Mayes and Muonasa began to occupy her mind.

At the end of the service on Muonasa's third visit to Dr. Haynes' church, the rector was waiting as usual at the door to say goodbye to his parishioners. Muonasa was next. Fortunately, because she did not want others to hear what she was about to say, the group of four following her out had been delayed in conversation so there was nobody immediately following her. As the rector smiled and started to shake her hand, Muonasa leaned forwards and in a half whisper said: "I would really like to talk to you sometime on your own. There is something troubling me. Is that possible?"

"Well, of course it is," he said, the smile becoming a little more earnest. "Obviously now is not the time. Shall I come round to your house and, if so, what day and time would suit you best?"

"No; thank you, but I think it would be better if I came to you. Would it be convenient if I met you here at church when there is no service?"

"Even better would be one of the church offices next door. People tend to come into church quite often, even when there is no service: some for quiet time; some to pray; and sadly some just to admire the architecture.   Still, better than not coming at all, eh?"   He resumed the broad smile.   "Let me meet you here and I'll show you where to go."   They fixed a date for a few days hence; Muonasa left; and the rector turned to say farewell to the group of four.

"Your first name is Muonasa; is that correct?" said the rector.

"Yes."

"It is a nice name."   He smiled.   "Where does it come from?"

"I am Nigerian.   Going back, my family is from the Yoruba tribe but my parents moved away from those traditions when they began to work in the city.   Well, to be fair, I think my grandparents had too.   I think that is one reason that my parents chose my name because it is not traditionally Yoruba; it is Igbo, which is a different culture."

"My name means: 'Spirit responds or advocates or answers or intercedes or intervenes or mediates'.   The main reason my parents chose it apparently is because they hoped that it would protect me from harm; well, a symbol maybe. But for me, the name contains the spirit; the name is part of me; so the spirit is within me and will always act for me.   But it has failed me."

"In what way, my dear?"

"I have an evil spirit within me that is going to kill me from a western disease.   I have to be given absolution from a priest and treatment from a British doctor. My own spirit Muonasa did not protect me."

Muonasa closed her eyes. *There he was again, as always when she cut out the real world. His face was staring into hers. Threatening or protective? Or both? The scissors took clippings from two more finger nails which he added to the small pile beside the makeshift canvas bed. The scissors moved down to below her navel again. Would it be just hair again - or worse? Relief as he moved back to place the trimmings on a small tufted pile beside the nails. She knew the blood would be last - and it was - but the film running in her head always stopped abruptly before that final sacrifice.*

"How do you know this?"

"I just know, Father. It has been made very clear to me."

And then her own father: "Fear God but never fear Man." How many times had he said that? As usual, the question shouted within her head, echoing from the insides of the bones of her skull: Why have you done this? Why have you put yourself into the hands of someone you know you should not trust but are now under his control? And worse - you now have to reconcile yourself with God as well.

Faith in God. Yes, all the hours she had spent kneeling in the choir pews, carrying the sacraments, watching her father down in the congregation, singing the praises. At home, the grace before dinner, the family bible readings after supper. And believing it. And still did. Why go to that man?

But he had told her. Some things no-one, even Christians, understand. Her faith was intact - but he could add to it, nurture it, embellish it. His work would lead her to a new promise, a new life, a healing. Her faith had not led to her illness; her sins had not caused it; something had passed through her spiritual safety net and embodied itself within her. A new spirit. A different spirit. A spirit not always recognised by God or priests. But he could rid her of it, although he would need the priest's help. But the priest could not do it on his own, which is why he, her new mentor, had to be with her during her absolution and indeed at all times. Without sacrificing any of her life, family or beliefs, he could dispel the malign influence and return her to her goodness. But there was a price.

"Yes, it has been made very clear to me."

"Please tell me from where this idea has been implanted in your head. I want to help you and, with God's help, I will. But I need to understand more. Come, my child, please try."

Is lying to a priest a sin, even when done to prevent greater evil? She could not tell the truth, that much was clear. Even whenever she thought of doing, his face came back, the face with the staring eyes, the sickly grin.

"The truth is, Father, that I am possessed by an evil spirit and also have a disease that may be curable but I need to see a specialist. I am taking steps to deal with the disease but I need your help with the spirit. I consulted an Anglican priest in Nigeria - my whole family is devoted to the Church - and also a doctor but they both told me that they did not have the power to deal with the problem in Nigeria. Only someone with the necessary expertise could help me. As far as the disease is concerned, I had to see a really good qualified specialist, which I am trying to do. Regarding the spirit, I had to see someone in the Anglican church closer to God and that person could only be in England. I am here to seek your powers to rid me of the spirit, something they could not do in Nigeria."

"But why?" asked the rector. "In the Anglican church, we are all servants of God, whichever country we are in."

"I do not know," said the girl. "All I know is what I have been told and I have followed the advice to the best of my ability. Please help me."

He was there again, as before, but his sickly grin was broader.

"Let us pray."

The rector lay down a prayer cushion before her and another in front of him, facing her. They both knelt and bowed their heads. The rector laid an outstretched hand to each side of her temples.

He spoke: "Dear Father in Heaven, I hold before you one of your children, who is troubled. Please forgive her sins and, through the power of your Holy Spirit, free her mind of the anxieties and despair that currently occupy her. Please help her to reconcile her fears and release her mind to be open to Your will, as manifest through the life and death of our Lord, Jesus Christ. Release her to a full life in Your service, unhampered by the evils that pervade this earth, contrary to Your will. Send her from this place in the full faith and knowledge of Your love and compassion and bless her to strive for a world in which all your people are drawn to you through the gift of Your son, Jesus Christ."

"Lord, bless her and keep her. I ask you Father, in Your mercy, to hear and receive this prayer. Through Jesus Christ, our Lord."

"Amen."

"Amen."

Muonasa and Adebanke were together, sitting next to each other in Muonasa's room, drinking coffee. They had increasingly bonded with each day they had spent together, not just because they were both Nigerian and had both been duped into an alien lifestyle in a foreign country but also because neither had fully absorbed themselves in it, as some of the other girls had. True, none of the girls in the house would willingly have been there but some, out of a sense of emotional self-preservation, had decided it was their lot; they could do nothing about it and had gone along with it. For the sake of sanity, the two new friends had also consciously taken on an attitude of passivity but there remained within both a presence elsewhere, another purpose in life that would not go away, however desperate they realised their predicament was and however much they realised that it was unlikely to go away. For Muonasa, this was easier because she saw her life in the brothel as a necessary evil in the quest for an ultimate treatment for her illness. And she had corners of her mind that remained protected: Mark Haynes and her stone. Adebanke deliberately, as far as she could, maintained an attitude of superficiality.

"You said once that you had a way of switching off between clients or when you were feeling low," said Adebanke. "How do you do that? I just shut them out but I think you are a much more serious person."

"I have a magic stone," said Muonasa, reaching to her right side to pick it up before holding it in the palm of her left hand to show to Adebanke. "I just gaze into it and it takes me to a faraway land where everything is fine. It tells me that everything will be all right."

"It *tells* you?" said Adebanke, in a tone of incredulity.

"Yes, it tells me."

"What are you on? Muonasa, stones do not talk. At best, you've got a vivid imagination; at worst, you are going mad - assuming, that is, that you are not *really* taking something."

"No, I am not taking something, Adebanke. And you know that I am not. Neither am I going mad. Ordinary stones do not talk, obviously, but magic ones do. I am not the first person in the world to have a stone like this. There was a boy back home once who was given a magic stone by a woman he met in a wood. She had protected him from an evil spirit in a lake and gave him a stone that she fished out of a stream. He only had to ask the stone for anything he wanted and it would be given to him. He ended up very rich."

"Muonasa, I know that story, as indeed do many people in Nigeria. It is an old folk tale!"

"Many folk tales are based on fact; indeed, I might suggest that all of them are in some shape or form." Something was drawing Muonasa to gaze into the stone and hear the man's voice again but she knew the time was not right and resisted.

"Well, you might suggest it but it doesn't mean it is true," said Adebanke.

"We'll see," said Muonasa and put the stone back on the bedside table.

For the next thirty minutes or so, the two girls changed the subject of their conversation to more trivial issues and settled back into their harmonious and comfortable relationship. During a pause in their speaking, Adebanke became pensive, then asked: "You never told me the full story of how you came to be here. You said that you had to come to England and someone had promised you accommodation but you had no idea that you would be staying in a place like this.

But you never said why you had to come in the first place. Was it something to do with your brother here in London?"

"I needed some medical treatment that could not be provided back home. I'd rather not go into details because it's all a bit personal but I am seeing the doctor and everything is going fine."

"So you would be able to go home when it's finished?"

"Well, that's what I am hoping but, as you know better than I do, in order to get out of here and on a plane, I'd have to find some money. And Adedayo - and the rest - might just make that a bit difficult. But I could not stay in this life the way it is, once I have received all the treatment I need. It worries me that you suggest it might become impossible and my heart grieves for you. But I know that I will find a way one day. My stone will help me."

Adebanke sighed and was about to change the subject of the conversation again. But then she saw, beside the stone, the small leather pouch.

"Muonasa, what's in that pouch?" she said forcefully. Muonasa did not answer. After a pause, Adebanke continued: "You do not need to tell me because I know. That pouch was given to you by a juju man, wasn't it? We saw those kinds of things all the time in the village where I was brought up. There was a lot of juju. I'll bet your life I know what's in that pouch - or something close to it. Don't tell me; let me guess! Is it nail clippings, pubic hair, a flask of blood or, dare I suggest it, something worse?"

Muonasa was silent.

Adebanke stared at Muonasa. "Where did you get that stone?" she asked.

"I found it in the countryside."

"Who was this man who told you to come to England?"

"I told you. He said I needed medical treatment."

"But who was he? What else did he tell you?" said Adebanke, her voice increasing in desperation.

"He said I had a bad spirit inside me and he could help me get rid of it," said Muonasa in a tone that combined pride with confession.

"Muonasa, you are the victim of a juju spell!" cried Adebanke, gazing back at the pouch, eyes wide open and her face aghast with horror. "He took you through some sort of ritual, didn't he? Well, didn't he?! The good news is that I don't believe a word of what these guys peddle about but the bad news is that you might!" Adebanke shut her eyes and shook her head in anger and frustration.

Neither of the girls spoke for several minutes. Muonasa sat calmly, looking at the floor, feeling unusually at peace. Adebanke had her head bowed and was breathing heavily, almost to the point of hyperventilation, until she too settled, began to breathe normally and looked back towards her friend.

She spoke gently. "Muonasa, my friend, you have to rid your mind of these ideas. These men are evil and use you for their own purpose. I feel bad enough that I was duped but so much more for you because this man, whom you trust, has not only deceived you, like me, but is controlling your mind and using you for his own evil purpose. I beg you, for your own sake, abandon this perverted plan that you have for nothing good will come of it. We can find you some money somehow; then just get on the plane, go back to your family and forget that all this ever happened."

"I can't," said Muonasa.

Later that day, when Adebanke had returned to her own room, Muonasa felt the call to the stone once more. As usual, she sat on the edge of the bed and cradled the stone in both hands. After gazing into it for a few minutes, she closed her eyes. She expected to see the green fields as she had before, but, on this occasion, her blinded vision was occupied by the face of a smiling, middle-aged man with vertical scars down both cheeks. He was wearing a close fitting white cotton hat and a necklace of red and white beads.

She gasped in recognition. *Why was he here now?* She had largely managed to suppress the recurrent, spontaneous images of his face that so regularly precipitated feelings switching between threat and protection but all the time controlling. But she had not forgotten him; how could she? He was the architect of all that was now taking place, a journey that began with the rite, the instillation of the spirit. That rite would stay in her memory for ever: the nail clippings, the trimmings of pubic hair, the sample of blood. But he had said it was necessary and she had believed him.

The face spoke: *Don't be in a hurry to go home, Muonasa. You've barely settled in and have a lot still to do. Remember the reasons why you set out on this adventure: you have to get your illness treated and that bad spirit removed from your soul. The good spirit that I gave you is going to support you all the way through; that much I can promise. You have made a very good start; you have set up a good relationship with your doctor and I would encourage you to pursue that to its fullest extent. You have also met with the priest, which is good, but you have more to do there. You need to get into his inner self and show him what you need him to do; that is, to get him devoted to your problem, as the doctor now is, and work with you to achieve the ultimate end, which can only be good for you, for all your family and for all your people. The role in which you now feel embroiled is a necessary means to an end. Trust me and your future is secured.*

The tenor of his voice, the poetry of his words, his countenance came together to generate a sudden and profound sense of calm in Muonasa's mind again. The fear that she had experienced when recounting her problems to the priest some time earlier and which had recurred at intervals now seemed a distant memory. Yes, something was working; she had set off on her journey under the direction of her spiritual advocate in Nigeria with compulsion but also dread; now the direction seemed more secure and much less unnerving. She vowed to continue, whatever the cost, until happiness came her way. She could then return to her family in the secure knowledge that all would be well thereafter. And she would gain a renewed relationship with her brother. Adebanke was kind but she did not understand.

She opened her eyes; the face disappeared; and she replaced the stone on the table.

Chapter 6

Amy was sitting in her bedroom on a mahogany carver chair, next to a small, circular, Regency pedestal table, her favoured place for texting her friends in private. Like most teenagers, she had had a virtual army of textees who occupied her for a large part of each waking day. Over the last year or so, however, she had discarded most of them and confined her electronic messages to just one, Lucy, who was happy to reciprocate.

They had gone through the usual daily interchange of banality before moving on to thoughts, ideas and observations that would seem increasingly bizarre to most rational observers. And they had their lives to plan.

As usual, each expressed to the other their concerns that had occupied them since the last text. Some subjects were dropped quickly, either because of reassuring words from the other or perhaps in spite of it. But others would recur over and over, their persistence not necessarily bearing any correlation with the objective nature of their severity. The two would alternate their roles, one the deliverer of anxiety, the other the appeaser, the switch in position occurring randomly. Whether either gained therapeutic benefit from these activities is dubious but they continued.

Amy cut short Lucy's exposition concerning the lack of understanding shown by either of her parents at the fact that Jake, her latest boyfriend, had failed to communicate for the last three days and seemingly had gone into hiding or disappeared off the face of the earth to tell her about Muonasa.

Amy did not know how she found out that her father was having an affair with a black woman, she explained, but she just knew it. Lucy was not only satisfied at her friend's conclusions but also horrified at such betrayal by a supposedly loving man, not only to his wife but also his daughter. In repeated texts, they amplified Amy's suspicions into an established truth that served to underline their mutual distrust of the world.

They decided that they would meet up at Lucy's later in the afternoon.

"Got the gear?" texted Amy.

"Yes," was the reply.

"Anyone about?"

"No."

Amy arrived at Lucy's in a fluster. She moved quickly through the door after Lucy had half opened it, checking first who was knocking. They ran up to Lucy's bedroom where she had already prepared the goods, albeit still hidden in a drawer. She took out the silver foil, a metal spoon, cigarette lighter and a small, plastic bag of white powder. Before long, their inhalation of the vapour from the liquidised powder had removed all their cares, made the angst-ridden texts of that day redundant and a distant memory and settled them both into a world of dream-like peace from which they felt they could never return.

But return they did. Eventually, Amy was able to shake off the residual drowsiness and return home. The thoughts that occupied her earlier in the day were not as bad but they were beginning to be. She shuffled into the sitting room.

"Where on earth have you been, Amy?" cried her father, in a mixture of anger, frustration and relief.

"Lucy's," said Amy, gaze fixed towards the floor.

"You've been coming home late too often these days and it's always from Lucy's. What is going on? It's only a day or two since we had a long discussion about your problems - your sadness - and I thought we had made a plan. Is Lucy a part of the things we talked about? I need to know, Amy, if I am going to be able to help you."

"I'm late, that's all. Sorry."

Amy and Lucy had spent more time together than the parents of either of them realised. The study afternoons provided by the school for the sixth form were a godsend and, in Amy's case, another excuse to retire to her bedroom was provided, in name if not by cause, by her recurrent migraines. She knew that there would be difficulty in maintaining this deceit but neither of them planned to continue their adventures for much longer. It was just a bit of fun, after all. And it wasn't really lying, was it? What seemed like lying was just an instrument of escape, escape from those who threatened her and her life. Those such as Muonasa. And then there was the problem of the money.

But for now, these things were less important. Amy slumped into the armchair beside the log burner, which fortunately her father had earlier stoked into full blaze so soon her shivering began to cease and her goosebumps receded. Her drowsiness returned.

"Amy," persisted her father, "tell me the truth. It doesn't all add up."

"What's going on?" said Becky, as she bustled into the room, alerted by her husband's raised voice.

"Well, as you can see," said Mark with a fake smile, "Amy has finally come home and, as you may have noticed, she is late.   You may recall that dinner is ready and you were wondering if we would have to eat without her. I was trying to find out why."

"Mark, leave her alone," said his wife, moving towards her daughter and enveloping her round her shoulders with her left arm, half smiling into her face.   "You know that she has not been feeling well recently.   Maybe we need to give her some space. We all had a long discussion about it, didn't we, Amy?" she said, moving her face closer to Amy's, slightly bowing her head and increasing the breadth of her smile.

"Yes," said Amy.   "We did."

"So where have you been?" persisted Mark.

"At Lucy's.   I told you."

"Doing what?"

Amy roused suddenly from her stupor, sat back, clasped her arms to the sides of the chair, raised her head and, with wide eyes, stared at her father.

"Well, probably more innocent things than you do when you find yourself alone with another female!" she screamed.

"What on earth are you talking about?" said Mark.

Amy thrust her head further forward and opened her eyes even wider.   "I know what you're up to," she shouted, "and it's disgusting!   Is it true that men are all the same?   You've no consideration for me or Mum!   You just think you can get away with anything and nobody will find out or, if they do, they won't care.   Well, I'll tell you, I have found out and I do care.   I care because I hate deceit and I hate infidelity and I hate how you could cheat on my mother."

"Amy, this is enough!" said her father.   "There is no truth in what you are saying and it is clearly a figment of your imagination.   I am not prepared to listen to it."

Becky went quiet and pensive for a minute or two. As Amy calmed down and began to doze in the chair, she turned to Mark who was standing motionless, lips clamped together, staring at his daughter.

"Where has this come from Mark? Can I assume there is no truth in it?"

"Of course there is no truth in it!" he replied in an aggressive whisper. "It's obviously part of her mental problems and frankly I find it difficult to cope with."

"*You* find it difficult to cope," said Becky. "What about her? Why are you so good at managing other people's problems and so useless at dealing with those close to home?"

"Because his mind is somewhere else," said Amy, now awake again. "Probably with that black woman."

"A black woman?" said Becky with an air of surprise, renewed interest and slight distaste. *Why would her daughter make up something like that?* she thought.

Mark sighed heavily and turned on his heel. "Shall we go and have dinner?" he said wearily.

"I'm not hungry," said Amy.

"Come on, darling, just try and eat something," said her mother.

"OK," said Amy, now more awake. She smiled and followed Becky into the dining room.

But she did not look at her father, who seemed excluded from the ensuing interactions between her and her mother.

Mark Haynes never wanted to force his daughter to go to church, even though he was a strong Anglican. He had tried to pursue a policy with her of leading by example and hoping that she would follow. Apart from the odd short-lived childhood or adolescent tantrum, she had complied. Mark, Rebecca and Amy Haynes, arriving together ten minutes before the onset of the service and taking their usual seats on the front pew, was a familiar sight every Sunday at their local church. Over recent months, however, Amy's attendance had been more erratic, partly due to her absence with alleged migraine, and partly because she simply refused. When she did choose to attend, her concentration was more intermittent and, at times, she would seem to switch off for brief periods for no clear reason.

Since the day that Muonasa had first appeared at their church, Amy's attendance had been much more consistent. Muonasa too had settled into the congregation and was generally welcomed although one or two members had felt the need to share with their friends the observation that she was the only black woman at the services.

Muonasa usually occupied the same seat at the back of the church that she had taken the first time she came. She was aware that she was different - in a number of ways - from the others there and did not want to push her presence too rapidly. Furthermore, she gained almost as much of an emotional lift from seeing Dr. Haynes' involvement in the service as she did from the service itself.

Amy's concentration remained intermittent. Whether a lapse in attention caused her to gaze around the church or whether the desire to explore her surroundings came first was not obvious to those who noticed but her gaze always fell on

Muonasa, whom she studied with such a penetrating intensity that Muonasa had to look away. Under normal circumstances, Amy's behaviour would have prompted Muonasa to find another church. But Dr. Haynes was here.

At the end of one of the services, as the congregation was making its way towards the refreshments, Rebecca noticed Muonasa waiting to leave her pew and looking towards Mark. She moved closer to her husband so no-one else could hear.

"Is that the woman Amy was referring to?"

"Which woman?"

"The one she says you are having an affair with."

"How should I know?" blurted Mark, prompting his wife to urge him to lower his voice for fear that Amy, who was following behind, would hear. And then, in an irate whisper, he added, "Can't you see that this woman and my supposed affair are all in her mind? I am not making more of a fuss about this because I am hoping that the treatment she is receiving from the psychologist will soon bear fruit and not only will her mood improve but her silly ideas, including this one, will disappear."

"Well, maybe, but I have to say that woman does look very interested in you."

"I have told you that she is a patient of mine. I cannot, for reasons of confidentiality, tell you more, not least because, if indeed Amy is fixated on her, God knows what she would do with any information she gleaned from me."

"Please don't blaspheme, Mark. As a woman, I know that the way she looks at you conveys an unhealthy interest - beyond the professional I would say."

"Well, thank you. I will watch out for it," he said abruptly. "If indeed there is any truth in what you say, which frankly I doubt, then maybe she has developed transference."

"What deep psychiatric phenomenon is that?" said Becky, with a tinge of sarcasm. Although Becky did respect her husband and the work he did within his speciality, she did harbour thoughts that the whole field was a lot of mumbo-jumbo, glorified and turned into a pursuit of respect by the use of fanciful and unrealistic theories concerning the operating of the human mind. Occasionally, she could not avoid a hint of that disquiet showing through.

"It's s a process whereby a person uses an object or more often a person as the focus for repressed emotions, for example from childhood."

"I see," said Becky, allowing herself a brief unvoiced resurrection of her scepticism. "Well, no doubt we will find out in due course."

Becky was not naturally jealous but she was aware that Mark had had one affair not long after Amy was born. Yes, she told herself, it was very probably precipitated by the new arrival and the disruption to their own close, almost insular, relationship that had lasted for ten years before another person demanded a share, particularly of her affection. And Mark was very busy at the time, trying to forge out a career. Nevertheless, it did indicate, she reflected, that he was capable of infidelity, something that she would never consider for herself, not least because of her Christian faith.

Since that affair, she had satisfied herself concerning its reasons; they had talked it through and their relationship returned rapidly to its previous strong state. She had felt no further disquiet. So, she wondered, why did she have to admit to herself that now she did feel some unease?　There was something about Muonasa that she could not define but she did not like it.　Maybe had she been aware of Muonasa's new employment in London, she could have put her feelings down to a strong sense of disapproval at even the possibility that her husband could have any kind of relationship with someone like that.　But, at that stage, she did not.　And, if she did, she would have been fooling herself because the origin of her concerns, even though she could not define them, lay much deeper.　Somewhere in her emotional soul stirred a feeling that this black lady was capable of exerting some kind of power over Mark, by means that maybe no-one could establish.　Her conscious mind dismissed all further thoughts of Muonasa and she continued with the activities that were more familiar to her, mixing with friends and looking after her daughter. So her anxieties settled.　For the present.

Muonasa had finished her day's work, cleaned herself up and changed her clothes.　Over the last few days, at this time of the afternoon, she had taken to going over to the window, surveying the scene, and playing a mental game of guessing which of the street life was about that day, who was likely to appear and whether any had taken any further steps towards self-destruction or destruction of others.　On this occasion, there was no drunk and no black Mercedes but, over in the archway at the end of the road, she glimpsed the familiar figure of the man in the hoodie.　She had already learned that, sooner or later, someone would turn up, hand over the cash and receive what she assumed was a packet or two into their clenched palm, which they would rapidly secrete away into the nearest convenient pocket. But who would it be this time? The anorexic looking man? The grey complexioned woman who looked about sixty but was probably half that age? The bearded man in a beanie hat with flashing eyes? Sad, she thought for a moment, that one of the few ways in which she could interest herself these days was by speculating on the person next in line for another episode of self-poisoning - but that's how it was.

As she continued to look at the man, she noticed something moving in her right field of vision. She turned her head and saw a teenage girl of smart appearance walking down the road. Some sense of familiarity caused her to look more intently although her rational mind doubted that any recognition would follow, least of all in this neighbourhood. Despite the early fading light of autumn, she gleaned enough of the girl's features, posture and general demeanour to dispel the doubts of her reason for there, walking alone in an alien part of London, was clearly Amy Haynes, the daughter of her consultant. *Yes,* thought Muonasa, *I have seen that persona often enough in the company of her parents that I can be sure: that is Amy Haynes and I would stake my life on it. But why was she in this area and where was she going?* Geographically, it was not far from her home but it could have been on a different planet as far as the features, the people and the lifestyles of the two regions were concerned. She was obviously on her way to somewhere - a class, a party, some sports arena, perhaps - and maybe this was somehow a short cut. Muonasa had almost reached the point of realisation that her speculation had gone far enough and she would probably never find the answer - unless it came out in conversation at church - when Amy stopped in front of the man in the hoodie. A few words were exchanged before Amy went through the ritual that Muonasa had now seen a number of times with other people in that situation. The goods were secured in Amy's pocket and she began to walk away.

An immediate and frightening sense of awareness overpowered Muonasa and she began to tremble. *Quick, quick, Muonasa!* Her bedroom door was left half open as she raced down the stairs, stumbling over the last two and breaking her fall against the hall radiator. She burst through the front door onto the street and looked to the left but could see nothing. Shifting her gaze to the right, she saw the girl about a hundred yards further down, quickening her pace. *Thank God!* Muonasa ran and caught up with her target just as she was about to take a turn towards the underground station. With her hand on Amy's shoulder, she abruptly halted her progress and half turned her towards her.

"Amy, it's me, Muonasa, from church. What are you doing?"

Amy glowered. "I know who you are; you don't need to tell me!" she said and began to walk away but Muonasa drew her back again.

"Amy, what are you doing? I know what goes on around here; I know what that man is selling. You cannot get mixed up in all that stuff! Tell me I am wrong!"

"What I will tell you is that what I do is none of your business. Do you live here?" she said, scanning the street with her eyes and gesturing with her arm.

"Yes," said Muonasa, "and I have seen what that man does. You may not think much of me, Amy, but I think a lot of you and your family and it concerns me a great deal that you might be getting caught up in something that can never do you any good and which you probably cannot handle."

"Well, I know you think a lot about *some* of our family - one member, to be specific - and it's so touching to think that you know so much about me when we have hardly spoken. And I know about you, probably a lot more than you realise, and now discovering that you live - and, I guess, work - on this street confirms what I already knew. You are nothing better than a cheap prostitute and in no position to lecture me on anything and certainly not what I do with my spare time!" She broke free from Muonasa's hold and marched off towards the underground station. Halfway there, she turned back and shouted at Muonasa, who was motionless where she had stood, "And you'd do well to keep yourself to yourself and stop destroying our family or who knows what might happen!"

Amy stayed where she was, watching Muonasa as she turned and returned to her house, and carefully noted the address as she passed through the front door.

Theresa Mayes had gone home after the party deep in thought. That daughter of the Haynes, Amy, had something deeply disturbing about her but Theresa could not yet decide what. But she knew that she would love to explore her mind, her spirit, a challenge that felt irresistible. Theresa prided herself on her experience. She had met people possessed by demons, others wanting contact with lost ones in the spiritual world, those troubled by the normal albeit inappropriate anxieties of living in this nonsensical world and some whose perceptions of this life and the spiritual world outside of it had been distorted by drugs or other artificial ways of changing reality. But she had managed to draw back so many people to the world that she knew: one with intimate contact of existence outside of this earth. She desperately hoped Amy would contact her. But, for now, she had to achieve her own peace. On arrival home, she did not delay in settling into her usual route to relaxation. She lay on a canvas mat, head supported by a small pillow, closed her eyes and let her mind drift to where it wanted to go. After about thirty minutes, she returned to the mortal world, pleased at where her spirit had just visited.

The next morning, Theresa awoke late but fortunately had no client booked until eleven. Her client arrived at ten past: a girl, Sharon, aged twenty-six whose mother had died prematurely six months earlier at age fifty-two. Sharon was three months pregnant.

"She was my age when she had me," said Sharon, "and now I am pregnant too. I believe that the baby I am carrying is a resurrection of my mother - in fact, I know it - but nobody will listen to me. My boyfriend barely speaks to me any more and my family thinks I am mad. They pressed me to see a doctor, and I did, but he told me it was all a symptom of a normal grieving reaction and I would get over it. He said I could take antidepressants but it wasn't advisable because I was pregnant."

"So what do you want from me?" asked Theresa.

"A friend said I should see someone like you to sort it all out with my mother - what she wants me to do when she is born, and so on. I found your name amongst a list of spiritualists."

"Well, I'm not a spiritualist as such but I hope I can help nevertheless."

Theresa spent several minutes in discussion about Sharon's life, her relationship at different stages of her life with her family, particularly her mother and, more recently, her boyfriend. She then coaxed Sharon into meditation. Theresa told her to close her eyes, relax her whole body and breathe gently but deeply for a few minutes. Under Theresa's guidance, Sharon then shifted her attention to different body parts, focussing on that part alone and feeling it expand and fill with energy, almost to the extent of seeing it glow with light. Eventually, after more direction from her mentor, Sharon entered a trance-like state in which virtually all awareness of the outside world was removed and her attention was focussed upon the spiritual planes.

"Now, put your question to your mother," said Theresa softly.

"Mum," said Sharon, "what am I to do when you are born? You are my mother but you will also be my baby. How can I treat you as both at the same time?"

The two women sat in silence for what seemed to Sharon to be a very long time with no response.

"Again," said Theresa. Sharon repeated the question.

As they continued, Sharon felt herself slipping into an even deeper sense of unawareness. From time to time, Theresa, in an increasingly soft voice, prompted her client to pose the question again. On one occasion, as Sharon did so, Theresa began making soft, low-pitched murmurings from deep in her throat, ostensibly to maintain the trance-like state.

Suddenly, after the exercise had continued for perhaps half an hour, Sharon sat bolt upright in her chair, opened her eyes wide and cried out: "Oh my God! Oh my God!" and then, slumping her head forwards into her hands, "Was that her speaking or you?"

"Nothing to do with me," said Theresa, "except in helping you to get an answer to your question."

"Thank you; thank you so much!"

"What did you hear, Sharon?" asked Theresa.

Sharon was excited. "I heard her say it would all be OK. She said that we all change physically as our lives move through different spheres and I should focus on my child as a baby. The spirit of each one of us never changes but the form in which it is contained often does. She said I should just carry on as normal, just as if I had had any other kind of baby. Most people do not even consider which spirit is inside their newborn so neither should I."

"And does that make you feel better?" said Theresa. "Does that answer your question?"

"Yes, yes so much!"

"That's good," said Theresa gently. And, after a pause, "Maybe it would be good if we pursued your relationship with your mother in her new form a little more. Would you be happy to meet up again?"

"Oh yes, thank you!" said Sharon. Theresa smiled with deep inward satisfaction.

"Theresa Mayes, Spiritual Counsellor, 6 Pimlico Mews, Islington." Amy had read those details almost every hour of the four waking days since the party. She had dialled the telephone number three times and hung up before it rang;

many more times had she thought about calling but didn't. *Theresa Mayes, Spiritual Counsellor.....Spiritual Counsellor.......Spiritual....*

Amy went back to the bedroom and lay on the white, cushioned quilt, closed her eyes and hoped that this time for once the visions would not return. But they did.

Streaks of white light cascaded down before her eyes, like rocket fireworks in reverse. After a few seconds, the streaks of light parted to reveal an awesome darkness, somehow much blacker than black itself. Although nothing was visible, she sensed a presence in that void - a real presence, a threatening presence, one that seemed to laugh without making any noise or sign - and one that was addressing her and her alone. As with every time before, she knew that the being, ghost or spirit, whatever it was, was directing her to act and it was communicating death. And communicating it to her. But was she then to die? And, if so, how? And when?

A being, a ghost, a spirit - yes, a spirit! And then the curtain came down on the vision, as it always did but, this time, she did not see the swirling blood-red clouds that had formed the last act of all her previous visions but instead a poster, depicting simple words in bold type: Theresa Mayes, Spiritual Counsellor, 6 Pimlico Mews, Islington. *Spiritual Counsellor.......Spiritual....*She rose from the bed and moved back to the lounge.

This time, she did not hang up.

"Can I help you?"

"I hope so."

Two days later, Amy was banging the heavy metal knocker on the front of the oak door.

"Do come in; how lovely to see you again!" said Theresa.

"Thank you," said Amy, as she shuffled into the hall.

After a few more pleasantries, the two were seated opposite but close to each other in Theresa's sitting room, which immediately appealed to Amy because of its minimalist style: a fairly modest room, with four small but adequately comfortable tub chairs, one chest of drawers, one bookcase, two mirrors and one painting. A small, square window, lined with white, cotton curtains looked out to the road. Amy examined the picture, a print of Dali's "The Persistence of Memory", until Theresa broke her concentration.

"I hope you did not mind my intrusion at the party but I couldn't help sensing your distressed state. What I do for a living, and have done now for many years, has given me almost a radar to pick up problems when I see them, even before people have said very much."

"No, that's fine," said Amy. "I am glad that you did."

"Good. I am glad too. Let's see if we can work together on what is troubling you and produce a solution."

For the next hour, the two engaged in deep conversation. Amy found it easy to express herself to this erstwhile stranger while Theresa had no difficulty in latching onto the innermost emotions of her new client. Even within that short time together, she explored Amy's childhood and relations with parents, friends and school. She listened attentively to Amy's account of the spirit that seemed to communicate with her and told her that she would be able to rid her of it but first she had to create in her a peace of mind. Amy had no doubt that a bond had been created and agreed without hesitation to a further meeting. When she raised the question of payment, she was reassured when Theresa told her not to worry at this stage and that no doubt something could be sorted in the fullness of time.

Theresa gave Amy some exercises to carry out at home. At least once each day, and preferably twice, she had to lie on her back in a quiet and dark place away from other people, knowing that she would not be disturbed. She had to let her body relax and mind go blank for several minutes before allowing her attention to switch back on. She then had to focus on the things in her life that gave her the most pleasure and the greatest chance of escape from all her cares and woes. Amy felt confidence in Theresa's quiet and empathetic manner, even though her probing questions sometimes seemed a little intrusive. By the end of their first meeting, she found it easy to agree to Theresa's suggestions.

Keen to embark on the exercise programme, she went up to her bedroom immediately after her return home, thankful that no-one else was in the house who might ask what she was doing or otherwise disrupt her intentions. As instructed, she shut the curtains, lay on her back on the bed and closed her eyes. When the time came for her to focus her mind, her thoughts moved quickly over a number of commonplace scenarios that at one time had provided release - friends, boys, sex, alcohol - but they were all short-lived. None of them maintained an image for long against the blank canvas that Theresa had told her to prepare in her mind.

Only when the drugs appeared did anything persist. Cannabis, ecstasy, methamphetamine and cocaine made their appearance in turn on Amy's new mental stage, each lasting for longer than the one before. The final and star turn there was heroin, which lingered, as if in a persistent long soliloquy until the curtains closed. Theresa had asked her to use this exercise to define what, in her current life, gave her pleasure and escape from worry and stress. And there it was. Was this the conclusion her counsellor had expected? Amy imagined not but she had done as advised and would take the results to the next meeting.

When the last phase of the exercise was done, the conscious wakening, Amy sat on the edge of her bed and phoned Lucy.

"All set?"

"Sure, come over. It'll be just you and me."

Over the next three weeks, Amy had four meetings with Theresa, once each week for two weeks and then increasing to twice weekly. Amy's life was laid bare before her mentor in all its aspects but increasingly Amy felt able to display the more intimate and the more honest aspects of her life and feelings as Theresa's probing charm worked its magic. A lady who understands people, thought Amy; a lady who can work things out; someone who has my interests at heart. And so the bond increased. But the notion of dependency never occurred to Amy, even though it was happening. What she needed was a guide through these difficult times and all that mattered was that at last she had found one.

At their next meeting, Theresa asked about the results of the exercises. Now was the turning point; the one thing that had not yet been laid out was the drugs. Although it had been lightly touched upon at an earlier meeting, Theresa had chosen not to respond. But now Amy knew that, to maintain the support that Theresa had given so far, she would have to be honest about everything, in all its detail. Despite that knowledge, Amy recounted her story with hesitation, so that her speech at first came out in stutters.

"Try again, Amy. Just breathe slowly and tell me, one word at a time. You mentioned that you reached the point in the exercises where you focussed on the things that gave you relief and you said 'substances' and then you went quiet. What kind of substances are those?"

"Things I take. Probably things I shouldn't."

"Like what?"

"All kinds of things, really."

Amy now started breathing heavily and avoided eye contact. Never before had she shared her secret life with anyone except Lucy and to start now, even though she knew it was ultimately necessary, was something she would rather put off to another time. Like many of the difficulties she had to face in life, in fact. But Theresa would not let it pass.

"I would rather you talked, Amy, but I need to help you and I sense you are going to find this difficult. So I am going to be presumptuous, if and until you tell me I am wrong. Are we talking about drugs?"

"Yes," said Amy, starting to cry.

Theresa took her by the hand and moved closer. "It's all right, Amy. It's just another thing. We have now established that drugs give you some relief from the trials and misfortunes that life has imposed upon you. There is no judgement from me concerning that fact. We now just have to take it on board, along with everything else you have told me about you, and move along whatever route will be the best for you."

As Amy looked up, she saw Theresa's smiling face and a wave of relief spread through her. The fears ebbed away and a new channel of communication, wider than before, seemed to open up between them. She smiled in return and placed her hand over that of her mentor. Trust was something that had, in recent months, seemed to evade Amy but now that had changed. Her new contact seemed like an oasis in an emotional desert.

The two talked for several more minutes, reinforcing their mutual understanding. Then Theresa sat back in her chair and said, "Tell you what, Amy: you go away now and carry on with the exercises, reflecting on what we have achieved today. Just do exactly as you have done before. I will see you in three days and we can decide together on what is best for you next."

Back home, Amy did as advised. Twice each day, on her back, her attention focussed as it had done before, seeking out the things most important in giving her peace. Every time, it returned to the drugs, different from previously only in so far as the convictions were stronger. On her return to Theresa, she reported her experiences.

"That's absolutely fine," said Theresa. "You have explored your being and identified what is a part of your life. I imagine you may feel guilty about it because society tries to give us moral codes and ways of behaving that it would have us believe apply to everyone. And, dare I say it, your parents are perhaps guided by the same codes - so you feel even more guilty because you know they love you and you love them. But the truth is that each person is an individual, separate from all others, and it is that individuality that needs to be cherished. What is good for one person is not necessarily good for the next and, almost certainly, is not good for everyone."

"But I can't believe the drugs are doing me any good," said Amy.

"They are a part of you. Maybe, in the fullness of time, things will be different - and that's fine - but, at the moment, they are a part of you. We can work on the next step but, for the moment, let's just take things as they are."

Amy fell silent.

"Let's talk about practicalities," said Theresa, "because practical difficulties only make your emotional difficulties more intense. Where do you get your drugs from?"

"Well, I've been getting them from a well-known area - or Lucy does - but now there are problems because someone there has recognised me and knows my parents. I am frightened that she will tell them."

"Exactly my point!" said Theresa. "You can do without the added strain of trying to submerge your identity in a world where already you have problems in expressing it."

"But what else can I do?"

"If we agree that, for the moment, you carry on as you are, building up your mental strength, then we have to release you from the problems of trying to do just that. And there I can help you."

"How?"

"Well, supposing I got the drugs for you and gave them to you. You would have no need to put yourself through the extra strain of finding them, with all the worries that that entails - people recognising you, telling your parents and so on - then we could carry on our programme together and it would be just you and me."

"I would have to pay you."

"Yes, but I can do it for you at a far lower cost than you would find on the street. If you agree, we can work that out. But you will end up spending a lot less money and we would still have our times together. Come tomorrow and I will have the gear ready for you."

"OK."

Amy awoke with a start. The sheet covering her was drenched in sweat and she was trembling with cold. *"Yes, but I can do it for you at a far lower cost than you would find on the street. If you agree, we can work that out. But you will end up spending a lot less money and we would still have our times together. Come tomorrow and I will have the gear ready for you."* She tried consciously to relax but the shaking did not stop and the pattern on the wallpaper in front of her seemed to coalesce and change colour. After a few minutes, she settled a little but everything still seemed bright and unreal. Even the bedclothes on top of her appeared to change weight in cycles over the course of seconds.

Is this real? she thought, in a moment of insight. *Well, I can see it, feel it and think it so it must be. And what about Theresa? What did she say? 'Come tomorrow and I will have the gear ready for you.' Can that be true? Yes, sure; why not? I guess she needs a living just like everyone else. That might be my solution; let's go for it!* The wallpaper blurred; her vision turned to uniform grey; all sounds ceased and she was lost.

When she next awoke, one thought dominated her mind: *I need some gear.*

"Dear Mark,

I hope you do not mind me writing to you but sometimes it is easier to put one's thoughts on paper than to speak them to someone's face.

I just wanted to say how much our times together have meant to me. From the first time we met, I have felt a strong sense that you would create something in my wellbeing much stronger than I could have expected when I booked that appointment with you. I am so glad I did it. Because, although I know that whatever condition I have will still need treatment, I also know that my main route to a fulfilling future lies with you.

I do hope that you will continue in our relationship. I am not exaggerating when I say that I have gained more from you emotionally than I have ever from anyone else. Our rendezvous have changed my life and I relish each one and look forward with eagerness to the next. Together, we build something, certainly in me. I consulted you for treatment and you have provided that and more.

Thank you for wanting to take such an involvement with me. As always, I can barely wait for the next time we meet.

love Muonasa."

Rebecca read the letter over and over, six or seven times, focussing more and more on every word with each repetition.

"So now what do you think?" said Amy, with an undisguised mixture of aggression and self-satisfaction. Her mother did not answer but continued to read.

"Well?" said her daughter. "Was I right or was I right?"

"Where did you find this?" asked Becky.

"I told you. In Dad's printer tray."

"In what?" said her mother, looking up from the letter for the first time since it had been presented to her.

"In the tray that holds the documents when they have been printed out from the computer - otherwise known as the printer tray," said Amy, as if speaking to someone with learning difficulties but with less tolerance. "I found it in the printer tray."

"So who printed it out?" said Becky.

"Well, let's think," said Amy, lifting her head and stroking her chin. "It's Dad's work laptop; nobody else at home uses it; the letter is addressed to him; and it was printed out on his home printer from a folder entitled 'correspondence', which includes lots of other letters presumably scanned in by his secretary but all addressed to him. So I wonder who could have printed it out. By the way, none of the other letters of that date were printed out."

"How do you know all this?"

"Because I looked."

"And why did you look?"

"To find evidence that might just convince you of the obvious - that your husband and my father is having an affair with that black woman from church. And surprise, surprise, I found it! I hate him - but I hate her even more. How dare she inveigle herself into our family, wreck your marriage and totally destroy my whole life?"

"Amy, maybe you are reading too much into this. There might be a simpler explanation, And honestly, darling, how can you say that it has destroyed your whole life when you have everything going for you and a future to look forward to?"

"Reading too much into it?" shouted Amy. "Unless I am mistaken, it's not written in ancient Greek but plain English. And you forget that I knew something was going on long before I found the letter. And as for me - have you also forgotten that my life is a mess at the moment? And it's all down to her!"

"But Amy, to be fair, you had problems before you met her."

"Oh, thank you! Well, don't we all? As usual, you choose to be blind to the real world and manipulate the facts to suit your misguided optimism. If you can't see reason, I'm going. See you later."

"Where are you going?" said her mother with obvious anxiety.

"Nowhere," said Amy, "just to Lucy's."

Amy rose abruptly from the kitchen chair and, without further acknowledgement to her mother, ran upstairs to her bedroom. Sitting in her usual chair, she texted Lucy.

"Are you free?" Receiving an affirmative response, she added, "Got the gear?"

Following a further affirmation, she snatched her coat and hurried from the house. Within an hour, Amy was peaceful and dreaming again.

Chapter 7

It was agreed that they should have regular meetings, when Muonasa's schedule allowed; the rector promised that, as far as possible, he would make himself available at any time. About once each week, they met in a small room in the church offices, the rector taking careful steps to ensure that they were not disturbed.   As was usual now whenever she went out, Muonasa ensured that she had her stone with her.

They talked through Muonasa's early life in Nigeria, her parents, her brother and the Christian faith of her and her family.   Each session ended in a time of prayer, focussing on her spiritual welfare and the relationship with her family. Sometimes, at Muonasa's request, they prayed specifically for her brother, although the rector usually failed in his attempts to centre on some specific concern about him.

After three of four meetings, the priest spent some time exploring whether there had been any change in Muonasa's feeling.   When she reported that there had but many difficulties remained, he moved on to more practical issues that may be of assistance. She resisted, however, his enquiries about her day-to-day life until his persistence forced her to sidestep the issue. She put her hand on her stone. *More lies,* she thought. *Again lying to a priest. Will that undo all the good that we have achieved so far? Will God understand and forgive me?* But she felt that she had little choice.

" I am working as a cleaner around the houses and hotels where I live. It's simple and undemanding but hardly groundbreaking. Not like I had back home."

"What did you do there?"

"I had a good job, working in my father's retail business. My family was not badly off; we had a good life."

"So now you have less money and I imagine you have lots of outgoings: rent, food and so on, things that maybe before your family could help with. Am I right?"

"Yes, times are a bit hard and I miss their support although obviously not as much as I miss them."

"No, of course. But, Muonasa, we Christians are a family, wherever we are living, and we can rely on each other to help each other, not just spiritually but also practically. If someone in our midst is in difficulty, it is our responsibility in the larger family to do whatever we can to make their life easier, to relieve suffering. That was the fundamental of Christ's message: tend my sheep."

"Thank you."

"So, Muonasa, if you need something, you only need to ask and, within my power, it will be given. Let's get down to the practical: do you need money?"

Without thinking, Muonasa placed her hand in her pocket and felt the stone again, which she stroked between the tips of her fingers for a minute or two. She knew in her heart that, although her life was torrid, it was not money that would lift her out of it but something compelled her to say otherwise. As she continued to hold the stone, that compulsion increased and the content of her ensuing speech seemed to flow automatically.

"To be honest, it has been difficult and, if anything, is becoming more so. I do not know how long my treatment will take and I am having to pay for it all because I am not a citizen of this country." *But, Muonasa, they told you back home that your expenses would be covered, not least from the work that*

the organisers had found for you. You might not like it but they
said it would pay your way.

"Then we as fellow Christians are duty bound to help you. If our mission on earth is to love and support all our fellow voyagers through this earthly journey and prepare them for the glorious everlasting life that awaits us all through the medium of Jesus Christ, how much more do we owe it to those who have already received and accepted his message? Our brothers and sisters in this congregation and the neighbouring parishes have been very generous in their support for our activities and I have little, in fact no doubt that, like me, they would willingly provide a contribution from the church funds to help you in your need. With the grace of God, one day you will be back in a position where you can return the material compassion to those who find themselves in a position similar to that in which you now find yourself."

"I feel sure that is true and, believe me, when I do, returning your grace will be my priority."

"So, Muonasa, would an initial contribution of two hundred pounds be sufficient for your immediate needs? I hope it goes without saying that we will review these practical matters each time we meet, and, when further resources are required, then they will be forthcoming."

"Thank you so much, Father. I cannot tell you how grateful I am and how much I will owe you for ever, not just in monetary terms but in every aspect of care that you have given me."

"Just trust in God and all will be well. Now let us pray."

When Muonasa got home, she put her stone back in its resting place on the table, sat on her bed and thought. *Why did I take the money? True, I don't have more than the little to live on that Adedayo gives me but what in this glorious life I am now living would I spend it on? Something tells me there is a reason. Should I send some back home? Maybe; maybe that's it. Maybe that's the reason.*

Muonasa approached the next meeting with the rector in apprehension. As she settled into her chair, with the priest opposite her in his, she kept her right hand in her pocket around the stone because she knew that that would always give her comfort, whatever she had to face. She did not want to concentrate on the practical, least of all money, for she knew that her purpose there was a spiritual one. Although she determined not to speak of those matters, she had little choice for it was the rector who raised the subject about twenty minutes into their meeting and again her responses seemed to follow without her thinking.

"Now, Muonasa, we avowed to consider your welfare in all its aspects. We have so far talked through some of your spiritual needs - your relationship with your fellow travellers in Christ, those who have not yet responded to His message, your family, in particular your brother, and your dialogue with God. Those are, of course, the most important and we will return to them in prayer shortly. But, as I have said before, we also need to look after each other in earthly matters and my role is to look after you. I have decided, with the blessing of the church, to donate another two hundred pounds from our funds to ease your passage through your daily trials and enable you to concentrate on your spiritual welfare. With the grace of God, that will enable you to be free of the burdens that you feel you are carrying and which led you to me."

Something led Muonasa to suppress her rational objections. Instead, she asked, "You say 'with the blessing of the church". Forgive me for asking but is your generosity shared by the church members who have provided this money by their own sacrifice?"

"I do not need to ask them, Muonasa, firstly because I have been entrusted with the administration of this parish but secondly, and most importantly, I have no doubt in my heart that they would share my views. Believe me, my child, I have prayed about this a great deal and though I admit there have been conflicts in the messages I have received, it is something about meeting you that gives me no doubt that this is where I have been led." He smiled. "I am satisfied."

The next few meetings followed a similar pattern. Muonasa was anxious and sought comfort in her stone; her priest explored her spirituality and, she had to confess, enlarged it; she experienced progress; and he continued in his generosity. Still, she pondered on how to make the best use of the money he insisted on giving until she remembered that her brother would soon be back in Nigeria, would meet her mentor and would talk in depth about her situation. Despite her misgivings, she decided that the best way forward, for the greatest benefit for everyone, was to entrust the money to her brother with the request that he decide with her mentor how it could be most usefully and productively spent. Satisfied by her decision, she smiled inwardly and stroked the stone in the palm of her hand.

At a later meeting, about the time that she finally felt she had achieved some calmness in her soul, her priest declared that, while his mission to support her had not ceased, he was running into difficulties.

"To be honest, Muonasa, the church funds are now virtually replete. I have no qualms about how that has happened because I sense a soul in distress. But I am having problems. In order to continue to help you financially, I would have to resort to my personal funds, which, of course, I am more than happy to do. And indeed I will do that because something tells me it is right and compels me to do so It would help me, however, if together we could now develop a plan for your future. How long do you think you are likely to be staying in London? I understand that you may not know exactly and no-one is wanting to rush you out of here - indeed, we are blessed by your presence. I am thinking only of practical matters at this moment."

"Well, really only until I have finished my medical treatment and you feel that I am no longer troubled by my bad spirit."

"My child, we have done so much together spiritually and have prayed earnestly to God for his guidance and deliverance. Our lives are in His hands but I feel sure that He will have heard our prayer and will work through the power of the Holy Spirit to lead you to fulfilment in this life and beyond. But you must continue to pray that He will keep you on that track and help you to resist the temptations to divert from it. We are all sinners but are blessed with the redemption of those sins through our Lord Jesus Christ. So now that you have taken your concerns to God through the medium of his son, your mind can be free of those concerns, allowing you to focus on God's will for you in this world."

"Thank you so much. I am so grateful to you. I will let you know about the progress with the medical treatment"

"It is not thanks to me. It is thanks to God. I will, however, continue to pray with you for as long as you are in London and will pray for you in your absence thereafter. Let us meet again in a few days, perhaps after your next consultation with the doctor. Meanwhile, here is your next allowance." He took some banknotes from a drawer in his desk and handed them to Muonasa.

"Thank you." *Why are you taking this?* She held the stone for comfort. "Thank you very much." *Just add it to the rest. You've already made a plan.*

"So, is she giving you the stuff?" asked Lucy.

"No. She went back on the deal," said Amy.

"What do you mean?"

"I went round again and reminded her of what she had offered but she claimed to know nothing about it. I don't know why. Nasty bitch. She makes an offer and then, when I say thank you, yes please, I'll take it, she says she doesn't know what I am talking about. She really pissed me off, I can tell you. How can someone say she'll give something and then, next breath, say she didn't? Anyway, I've had enough of her."

"Amy, why would she do that?"

"Probably because the cops had rumbled her. She wanted to appear squeaky clean and so denied anything to do with what was pretty obvious to everyone. But that doesn't help us and that's exactly what she said she wanted to do - help us - or me anyway. Bitch. Anyway, now we are back to square one, paying through the nose for a bit of pleasure."

"So, how did you leave it?"

"That's exactly what I did - leave it. I told her she was a nasty old cow and walked out."

"But your folks thought you were going for treatment."

"Well, I was, but it didn't work."

"But that's not where they thought you were going. They thought you were going to some woman from the University."

"I did go there a couple of times and then told her I had to break off for a while. That's when I went to Theresa. But, after I said goodbye to the bitch, I contacted the University woman and said I wanted to come back. So that's what I am doing. Well, that's the idea, anyway. Mum and Dad agreed all along not to intrude and she said everything would be confidential so nobody is any wiser."

"And what do you do with her - the one from the University?"

"Not much. Most of the time I don't actually go but I don't think she cares. She said she couldn't achieve anything if I was not willing. So sometimes I turn up and we have a chat, just to keep things going."

"And she's told you to stay off the drugs?"

"Yes, of course. But she doesn't do any blood or urine checks or anything."

"But your parents think you go regularly? Don't they ask how things are going? Aren't they paying her?"

"They seem happy when I leave the house at the right time to get to her meeting but I don't think they have surveillance cameras everywhere so they never quite know, do they? And, yes, they ask about how it's going but I tell them it's fine, really helpful, feel we're getting somewhere, slowly of course - that kind of thing. And, as far the parentals are concerned, they seem happy when I talk about the treatment I get from 'her' without enquiring too much which 'her' I am talking about. And, as for paying, the folks give me the money for all the sessions but I only pay for when I turn up. The rest of the cash, for the ones I miss, comes in pretty useful." Then she laughed: "As you know!"

"What about the other woman you went to? Who's paid her?"

"The bitch? She didn't want anything. She said she wanted to help."

"Why would she then make you an offer of drugs but later withdraw it?"

"I don't know. Maybe she's deranged. Or just a bitch."

Amy's plan worked well for a while but neither of the two girls foresaw that their 'bit of fun' would escalate to become more of a drain on their resources than either could accommodate. "What are we going to do about money?" said Amy one day, as her mind returned from one of their trips together to a state where she could begin to think.

"I don't know," said Lucy. "I have almost drained all the money from my account and no doubt the folks will soon want to examine the statements again. They only allowed me the account as a test of my responsibility, as they put it. Almost all the money I earned from the holiday jobs has gone, not to mention Grandma's gift. I admit, Amy, I am worried."

"And I owe you a ton of money," said Amy. "I'm sorry that my lot are not that generous - or trusting, I am also sorry to say - although the money for my treatment did come in handy for a while."

"I think we had better stop the white stuff," said Lucy. "It was daft to start in the first place and we only meant to try it for a bit of fun. If we hadn't been drunk and that guy at the party hadn't offered it, we would probably never have thought of taking it. We've not taken it for long and I know it can be addictive, but, if we stopped now, we would be fine. We're already starting to do it more often and that's why we are running out of money."

"But that's all past history," said Amy, "and remember we were smoking grass before that. We've liked getting high for quite a while. Stop worrying; it's fun, as you said!"

"But we are going to have to stop pretty soon because we simply won't have the cash. Never mind what you owe me - I just haven't got much more."

"Well, I've got an idea," said Amy. "We just have to earn buckets of cash and then we can carry on!"

"Very funny," said Lucy, "and how exactly do you suggest that we do that? We are students, remember, about to go to university and I don't think the folks would take it very well if I told them I was going to give that up and go out and earn 'buckets of cash', as you put it. Quite how we would earn 'buckets of cash' in a first job, anyway, is another matter."

"No, we carry on as we are but, from time to time, we just do a little job that will keep the money supply going?"

"With 'buckets of cash'? Like what?"

"Well, I've found this website where guys are looking for a few favours, well let's say sex to be exact. We just have to satisfy their desires and the organisers pay us a load of money. We don't even have to make any arrangements. It's all done for us. We just turn up at the address they give us, do the necessary - for how long? - I guess an hour - and then go

110

home. Then we've got the money to keep having fun and cutting the crap from this world."

"Amy, are you serious?! That's prostitution!"

"No, it's not. Trust me, I know about prostitutes and their ways. Prostitutes spend all day of every day banging away with undesirables and giving their money to some pimp who controls them. Some of them, I have to say, also give their services to a select one or two without payment but that's another story. What I am talking about is just the occasional favour with guys selected by the organisers of this website and they guarantee hefty payment. They will even restrict our activities to the local area so we do not have to travel far. Come on, Lucy, it's just the occasional mindless shag. You've done that before, haven't you?   Like Micky Taverner, for example." She grinned and stared meaningfully at Lucy, who closed her eyes and turned away.   "The difference," added Amy, "is that this time you will be paid handsomely. Just lie on your back and think of England, as someone once said." Amy started to laugh. "They even supply condoms!"

"It's not funny, Amy," said Lucy.   "And, by the way, it's illegal because you are not eighteen."

"I will be in three months and anyway nobody's going to find out."

"How would you feel when the poor guy gets prosecuted for having sex with a minor?"

"Can you hear me, Lucy?   Nobody is going to find out! Anyway, I'm up for it," said Amy. "I like skunk and I'm willing to work for it. Think about it."

Lucy fell silent. After a few minutes, Amy spoke again.

"OK, well I owe you a lot. I will do it on my own until you see sense and feel ready to join me. In the meantime, my money can support us both, like yours has done so far."

"I'm not going to let you do it, Amy. I'm really not."

"That's very sweet," said Amy sarcastically, "but, first of all, you have no choice." Then, softening her tone, she added, "There's not much choice for either of us, Lucy. Can you see another way?"

"I have told you already - let's give up the stuff."

"And, as I have also told you, that's not what I am prepared to do! And, let me add, do you think you could actually do it? Speaking for myself, the gear is the only thing that gives me any relief from the horrible things that are out there - like that horrible black woman, who is plaguing my life and breaking up my family."

"What black woman?"

"Apparently, she is called Muonasa. She has come over from Nigeria and has been consulting my father for some mental illness. Now, she comes to our church, has stalked my Dad and now is having an affair with him! Not only that, but somebody at church told me she is a prostitute. So, if my father thinks it OK to sleep with a prostitute, what's wrong with his daughter following the same line?" Then, becoming more subdued, said, "But, as you know, and as I have said, what I am suggesting for us is nothing like as bad as that."

"Are you sure he's having an affair with her?"

"Yes, Lucy. For a start, I just know it; it must be obvious to anyone except perhaps a blind person. And, not that I need any other proof, there is also the fact that she wrote him a letter. Do patients normally do that to their consultants?"

"Maybe, Amy; I don't know and I'm not sure you do."

"Oh yes, I do!   And I'll tell you, writing letter to consultants is what they don't do!"

"Well, it's good to have a friend who is an expert in the goings on of the medical profession," said Lucy quietly and casting her eyes downwards.

Amy was seated in the middle of the settee with her mother to her left and her father in a separate chair to the right of them. Amy was looking at the floor, playing with her fingers and chewing on her lip; her eyes were darting from side to side. Her mother had her hands in her lap; she was blinking repeatedly, trying to hold back the tears; her father looked sombre but calm.

"Just tell us calmly, Amy; is it true?" said her father.

"You seem to know everything already so why are you asking me?"

"We need to know exactly what has been going on, Amy; otherwise we cannot help you. We've got to have all the facts. Please tell us what you have been taking and for how long."

"We love you, darling," said her mother. "You know that. If you have got yourself into some kind of a mess, we will still love you; we will love whatever, come what may.   But please tell us what has been going on. We've got to nip this in the bud and that's what we are going to do." She began to cry. "I couldn't bear the thought of you going down some slippery slope to your ruin and, for all I know, death."

Amy lifted her head and turned to look at her mother, eyes now still. "I'm taking heroin," she said quietly.

Her father lurched back in his chair. "Oh, my God! So it's true!"

"Why are you so surprised?" said Amy, voice now raised and glaring at her father. "Your informer has already told you that! For some reason, you just want to hear it from my own lips!" Her father remained silent.

"How long has it been going on? How did it start?" said her mother.

Quiet again, Amy said, "Like most of us, I started smoking weed when I was about fourteen and it just went on from there - speed, cocaine, a bit of ice and now this."

"Ice? What's that?" said her mother.

"Crystal meth," said her father dispassionately. "Powerful amphetamines." Turning to Amy, he continued, "How long have you been on the heroin?"

"About three months."

"Do you inject it?"

Amy had, by now, resumed her previous posture, gazing at the floor. "No, never. Only smoked."

"Where have you got the money from? How have you paid for all these drugs?" said her mother in a tone that mixed puzzlement and anxiety.

"Does it matter?" said Amy.

"Of course it matters!" said her father. "We don't want to add other problems to the ones we've already got."

"*We* have got?" said Amy, voice raised again. "I thought it was me you would worried about, not 'we'! But, of course, you don't want your precious reputation ruined, do you?"

"Amy, that really isn't fair," said her mother, putting her arm around her daughter's shoulders. "Your father is only worried about you, as I am. We just want to get all this sorted out as quickly as we can so we can go back to being a happy family together again."

"Well, the money comes from Lucy, if you must know." Then, turning to her father, she added in exaggerated sarcasm, "So all your worries about impending bankruptcy can now be laid to rest." And then, turning back to her mother, she continued, "And as for being one big happy family, I don't think that's very likely to happen, whether I'm taking drugs or not!"

"What on earth makes you say that?" said her father.

"Are *you* asking me what makes me say that?" said Amy. "You? You, who are doing everything possible to make sure we are not a happy family? Well, maybe not just you - maybe you together with that black bitch!"

"Amy!" said her mother, in genuine shock.

"We are not resurrecting that old story, are we, surely?" said her father. "I thought we had been through that last time you suggested it. Amy, it pains me to say this, but I fear that the drugs are affecting your ability to think straight. That's not a criticism - far from it - because I know very well how these drugs affect the mind, without the person affected necessarily realising it. I see it every day."

"It is not a figment of my imagination," said Amy indignantly. "The way she looks at you and you at her are not figments of my imagination. The letter she wrote to you was not a figment of my imagination. She is without any doubt a trouble-maker. Why else would she go to the trouble to telephone you to tell you that your daughter was taking drugs?"

"What are you talking about, Amy?" said her father. "Muonasa, if that is the person to whom you refer with the term 'black bitch'" - her mother sighed and shook her head - "has done no such thing. I - we - have had no communication by telephone or any other means from Muonasa about your drug-taking or indeed any other matter concerning you."

"Then who has told you if it's not her, might I ask?" said Amy.

"Well, since it seems so important to you," said her father, "I will tell you that it was Lucy. She was very worried about you and felt that she had to let us know to stop you running into further trouble."

"Like what?" said Amy anxiously.

"She didn't say but she was very worried about you."

Amy's temper suddenly flared and she stood up. "I don't believe a word of it! Lucy would never do that; she is my friend and I know her very well! She would *never* do that! Never! You are just trying to protect that black - that black - woman. You think she is so wonderful that you cannot keep your hands off her but she is just a manipulator. She wants you for what she can get out of you - and out of our family - and nothing more! With your blessing, she will destroy us! Well, let me tell you something - I'm not as stupid as you are - and I'm not going to let it happen. I'd rather see her dead first!"

She was about to run off but her mother leapt from her seat, grabbed her by both shoulders and turned her round to face her. Head bowed and eyes wide, she spoke almost in splutters: "Amy, you must not say things like that, however you feel! Just think for a minute - maybe your father is right! Maybe, just maybe - think about it - your thoughts are coming from the drugs and not from you."

"I'm not a fool, Mum, but you are! You cannot - or choose not - to see what is in front of your eyes! My father - your husband - is sleeping with that woman, who has some kind of curse on us! Oh, and by the way, she is a prostitute!"

And she ran off to her bedroom as Becky released her grip in shock.

Becky turned towards her husband. "Is that true, Mark? Is she a prostitute? Did you know that?" And, raising her voice, "Did you know that the woman who comes to our church, ostensibly to praise God, and who writes you lovey-dovey letters, is a *prostitute*? Tell me!"

"What I know about her and what I don't is a matter of professional confidence. I couldn't tell you even if I knew."

"Oh, how convenient! Especially convenient if you have something to hide! And the fact that you do not deny what Amy says about her would lead any sensible person to the conclusion that what she says is true."

"What's brought this on? I have nothing to hide. As I just said, I cannot comment on what I may know about her private life because that is confidential. But, just for the record - although I believe it's already recorded - I am not sleeping with her."

"Having an affair is bad enough - but philandering with prostitutes! Oh, please!" She began to cry. Mark stood and moved over to comfort her but she pushed him away.

"I'll tell you something, Mark: I am not going to allow some cheap trash to destroy my daughter! You've got to stop seeing her or I may do something I later regret! If you don't remove her from our community, our family and our life, then I will!"

"And how exactly do you propose to do that?" said Mark, scowling.

"Sometimes I hate you, Mark!   I'll do it somehow; I haven't yet worked out how. But I have enough to think about in sorting out my daughter without some tramp making her condition ten times worse!" She ran into the kitchen.

"*Our* daughter, I believe," said Mark quietly.

He stood in the centre of the sitting room in deep thought. *How could I not have realised? All that stuff about a spirit occupying her mind that I thought was some simple adolescent anxiety. And then the obsession with Muonasa. And the feelings of paranoia. I see this every day in patients on drugs. But I couldn't see it in my own daughter. Why not? I'll tell you why not, Mark - for the same reasons that you give to your patients who feel life has bowled them a wobbly that they couldn't see coming: because that's what life does and the answer is not to find out why it happened or why you couldn't foresee it but to work out how you are going to deal with it! And now I'm left with a deranged daughter who certainly won't get out of her convictions by any rational argument. And she won't agree to treatment for drugs, as long as she's convinced about this spirit, or whatever it is, of that I'm sure. Meanwhile, her mother - my wife - is becoming entrapped in the same web. Everything is going down the tubes. If only I could have seen this coming. But you didn't, Mark, you didn't! I never thought I'd be the sort of person who could end up in desperation. Yes, something has to be done to save my daughter, my wife, our marriage and our family. Something, yes indeed. But what?*

Amy had not been able to have a fix for three days and she felt lonely, even isolated. She had taken to her bedroom on the pretext of working on her laptop. She knew that she would not be disturbed before she decided she had done enough and the hour had advanced to her bedtime. But she had no energy to do anything. After a quick text to Lucy to express her feelings, she changed into her pyjamas and climbed into bed without waiting for a reply. *Haven't brushed my teeth*, she thought; *that would make Mum cross.*

After an hour's tossing about, she finally went to sleep. Then it started.

Sitting on a sandy desert, her eyes forced closed by the brilliance of the sun, she felt cold shivers running through her arms and legs yet her face was burning in the heat. The sweat that trickled down her face and fell in droplets from her chin felt like a slow, warm shower against the skin of her chilled limbs. When a shadow fell across her face, she was able to open her eyes but how she wished she had not for between her and the sun was a giant blackbird, twice her size, with its head bowed and beak pointing towards her, about fifteen centimetres away. She tried to close her eyes again but the muscles seemed paralysed. In panic, she looked to left and right and saw a passive audience of smaller birds, gathered around the giant in a semicircle. The blackbird's presence was menacing, threatening, a feeling soon confirmed when it began its rapid, pecking movements against her head and body. In vain, she shifted her face and limbs out of the line of attack but the blackbird seemed expert at anticipating her movements. Within seconds, her whole skin felt as if it were penetrated by puncture marks. She cried in desperation to the other birds around but they did nothing. Indeed, the smile that appeared across the face of the blackbird seemed reflected across those of the others. She lifted her head to the sky and cried again but louder. A shimmering appeared between two white clouds from where a voice seemed to come. She could see nothing more but there was no doubt who was speaking. "Stop being difficult, Amy; just stop it," said her father. When four or five of the smaller birds moved forwards from the nearest margins of the semicircle and began pecking at her legs, she screamed and screamed, louder and louder as the birds moved up the inside of her thighs, and her eyes closed involuntarily.

"Amy, are you all right?" shouted her mother, in distress at the bedroom door.

"Yes, I'm fine," said Amy as her open eyes took in the familiarity of her bedroom.

"Have you had a bad dream?"

"Yes, but I'm OK now," said Amy.

"Go to sleep, darling. Hope your next dreams are a lot sweeter!"

Her mother left. Amy was now conscious in reality but the blackbird and its friends seemed not to disappear.

Chapter 8

One day, Adedayo appeared at her bedroom door uninvited, as usual, a letter in his hand. Muonasa was still half naked; that did not seem to bother him but she hastily wrapped her only towel around her waist, which at least covered her lower half. She sighed in embarrassment and looked towards him in a clear display of indignity but he showed no reaction.

"A man came to the door this morning with this letter for you. He told me that he knew you would not be able to contact him so he would return this afternoon for me to give him your response. I will be downstairs; when you have decided what to say, let me know and I will convey it to him when he comes back."

Just before leaving, he added: "By the way, we want no funny business. So you know, we have no secrets here so I have read the letter. It fits with what you have told me, which is good, but do not try anything underhand because, remember, people are watching you and I do not want you to come to any harm."

The letter was from her brother.

"Dear Muonasa,

I knew, of course, that you were coming to London. I also knew that you would probably not be desperate to get in touch with me and, anyway, you did not know my contact details. Naturally, our family back home is anxious about you, as indeed am I, but they perhaps more so because they have not heard from you. So I thought I would make the move and try to satisfy us all about your welfare.

I took the trouble, and you may feel the presumption, of using some of the people I know to find your address from the immigration authorities; you will recall that you had to provide a residential address when you entered the country. I hope you do not mind and will ultimately feel that my invasion of your privacy was only for the good.

I should like to meet up with you to talk things over and hopefully renew a relationship we once had. I know that our parents would value that very much, as would I, and I hope you would too.

I understand from your landlord that your availability is limited but I believe you may be free on Wednesday afternoon, that is in two days' time. If so, perhaps we could meet then, say at two p.m. I would be happy to come to your house to pick you up and we could then go to my club, where we would be able to find a quiet place to talk.

To simplify matters, I said I would return this afternoon to learn your response, which will hopefully be in the affirmative.

Looking forward to seeing you.

Your brother,

Obaloluwa"

Muonasa had always been suspicious of her brother's motives, knowing how rigid he was in his outlook on life, but she was concerned at her inability to communicate with her parents and the tone of Obaloluwa's letter seemed so conciliatory and concerned that she was prepared to consider that his heart may have opened up to her concerns. She would have to be careful not to let him know or even suspect what she was doing and that would be difficult. But, on balance, it seemed worth the effort and she did have time to think of a plausible story. She decided to take up his offer of a meeting and conveyed her decision to Adedayo. Nevertheless, she awaited Wednesday afternoon with some trepidation.

They managed a part-spontaneous, part-formal, embrace on the steps of her house and a few noncommittal words before he gestured her into the passenger seat of his car. What he felt at that stage she was unsure but she did feel a definite, albeit hesitant, warmth towards him and pleasure at seeing him again. By the time they arrived at the club, the somewhat stilted and purely social interchange had developed more spontaneity, a few reflections on times past and even some laughter.

She knew her brother had done well since moving to London but she had not understood quite how well. In one vision, as she walked into the club lounge, the contrast between his life and hers was laid bare: she had been transported - literally in a fine car - from a world of degradation and threat to one of freedom, privilege and wealth: large, brightly lit windows, leather armchairs, antique period tables and waiters in attendance. To one side was a long, mahogany sideboard bedecked with plates of fine canapes, crystal glasses, carafes of spring water and bottles of wine. *How had he gained such a position?* she thought.

They settled into two chairs by the window, away from the ten or twelve other people, all men, who made sparse occupancy of the large room.   Finding somewhere distant from them all was not difficult. Once Obaloluwa had brought the drinks, hers a glass of water with ice, his a fresh orange juice with a twist of lime, they resumed their conversation.

She established that he was still working in the oil industry but had recently been promoted, which had allowed him to move to a larger apartment in a better area of London, closer to his office.   He had managed to secure a flexible contract, which he would like to believe was a reflection of his abilities, so he still carried out his own private work, which he could manage from home.   A lot of these dealings were with clients back home in Nigeria.   Yes, he said to Muonasa's enquiry, he was still very active in the church and had recently taken on the role of head of pastoral care, which meant that he could connect more with ordinary people in the community. He was vague about the Nigerian contacts but Muonasa let it pass because, after all, she barely understood what the rest of his work entailed.

It did not take long before the conversation shifted to her own life.   She sidestepped the general enquiries from her brother until suddenly he became more direct.

"Muonasa, what exactly are you doing? Be honest. I know the area in which you live and I know what goes on there. Not only that but I have made enquiries about the house you occupy and I know what goes on there too. Your landlord told me that you work there. I hate to say or even think this but I have to put it to you that you are engaged in something evil. I realise that you may not be doing what you are doing from your own choice but ultimately choice is in our own hands."

He leaned forward, grasped her by the arms, and looking

directly into her face, said: "Muonasa, are you working in prostitution?!"

His grip on her arms provoked the immediate thought in Muonasa of Adebanke, grotesque men and violence and she withdrew reflexly in fear.

"I was sent here on a mission and some things I have to do to fulfil that. That much I understand. But, no, I do not understand how it works. I just have to see it through."

"What do you mean, Muonasa? Is this a mission from God? Have you had some sort of vision or has it come to you through prayer? Or, dare I suggest it, from somewhere else? If so, we need to know. If you are involved in prostitution, that message cannot have come from God!"

"*We* need to know?" said Muonasa. "What has it got to do with you?"

"We are Christian people, Muonasa, and the 'we' includes you and me. There is nothing more important than our faith; I have set my life on it and I believe you have too. Even so, we are all subject to temptation, sin and false idols. What I have to do is to ensure that the faithful do not fall by the wayside. That includes all my Christian brothers and sisters but especially those who are my flesh and blood. Which means you."

"You know I hold the faith," said Muonasa quietly.

"Yes, I believe you do. But tell me how and why you have ended up where you are."

"I have worries; I have anxieties; I am seeing a doctor for them."

"Why here?"

"Because it's the only place that has anyone qualified enough."

"But, Muonasa, that cannot be true. There are lots of suitably qualified doctors back home who could deal with those sorts of problems."

Muonasa sat back straight in her chair. "Obaloluwa, do not be presumptuous! You know nothing about my problems and I would beg you not to comment on areas about which you are ignorant!" As she settled back, she added quietly: "I saw someone back home and this is what he advised me to do."

"Who did you see?"

Muonasa stood up abruptly. "A Yoruba man, if you must know! Obaloluwa, I do love you as my brother but sometimes you can be intolerably difficult. Can I go home now?"

As he stopped the car at the door of her house, he leaned towards her while she was still sitting in the passenger seat. "I am sorry if I have upset you. Will you see me again?"

"Maybe," said Muonasa and she got out of the car.

When she returned to her room, Muonasa took the stone from her pocket and looked into it. No image or voice appeared but, though she felt a little deprived, she felt warm, settled and comforted. Her mind cast back to the times as a young child, when she was sitting on her mother's knee, hearing stories. All sorts of stories and, yes, the story about the boy with the magic stone as well. It can indeed be that old stories are based on some sort of truth, she said to herself, although we may not always understand what that truth is and how it may express itself. That man in the country had told her always to keep the stone with her and now she could see the importance of that advice. It is good for me, she thought, and I will not let it leave my side.

Despite all that had happened in their earlier life, she was glad that she had made contact with her brother and, yes, she would see him again. *Maybe this is the start of the healing; maybe soon everything else will fall into place and she can go home, renewed.*

"Are you happy to go to the club again?" asked Obaloluwa as Muonasa settled into the passenger seat.

"Yes, of course," she said, smiling, maybe just a little artificially. "It was lovely."

They settled into the same seats at the club; the waiter brought them their usual drinks without asking and they began their conversation but this time it flowed freely, without fear, anxiety or aggression.

"You seem much happier - and settled," said Obaloluwa.

"I think perhaps I am," said Muonasa. " I am glad that we have met up again and, dare I suggest it, that it may be a regular thing. It seems we can have a better relationship in London than back home. If so, it must be a good thing that we both came here."

"Absolutely!" he said, squeezing her arm.

Over the next hour, she learned more about her brother's work in the oil industry although she admitted that a lot she did not understand. He seemed pleased to be able to share his lifestyle with his sister but really came alive when she asked about his continuing work back in Nigeria.

"Even though I am almost five thousand kilometres away, I am managing to make major inroads back home and I admit I am delighted! Since I have been here, we have created five new Christian parishes across the South-West of our country and there seems that nothing can stop the enthusiasm there. Of course, the money that I am able to put back from my admittedly hefty earnings here helps enormously but, despite that, there seems to be a movement that is unstoppable. I am so proud to have played a part in that progress!"

"Is it really so good or are you fooling yourself, maybe even just a little? There is still some resistance to Christianity from the traditional Yoruba clerics - well, a few of them at least. Will they not continue to resist?"

Obaloluwa reached into his briefcase and withdrew a handful of pamphlets. "Take a look at these," he said. "This is just some of the literature that is being distributed and which is being well received. Take them and, when you have some spare time, look at them prayerfully. If, in any small way, you feel able to help, please do but I know your opportunities are limited. Nevertheless, perhaps the most powerful thing you could do is to pray for us and them. But, yes, there is some resistance."

Muonasa took the papers and placed then in her pocket. As she did, her fingers rubbed across her stone and she felt happy.

But it did not last. Just fifteen minutes later, Obaloluwa abruptly changed the subject of their conversation.

"I have to return to something I spoke to you about earlier," said Obaloluwa. "And I beg you to give me an honest answer. Are you involved in prostitution?"

"I have already told you, Obaloluwa, that I have been given a mission to carry out to make me whole again. That is the most important thing in my life. Some parts of it are unpleasant, yes, but I realise that I have to follow it through, with all that that entails, whether I like it or not. I do not understand how it all works but I was told in advance that I wouldn't. Some things can seem shocking at first and, to be honest, I suppose they do but, if it works in the end, that's all that matters. And I can say that some things do seem better already. So why give up now?"

"Well, it looks as if I am not going to get a straight answer from you, Muonasa, but perhaps I don't need to," he said dismissively. "Let me tell you this, as I think I have told you already: I know what goes on in that area where you live; I know what goes on in that street; and I know what goes on in that house. And, since you refuse to deny it, it seems I know what you do too."

"Even if what you say is true, what is wrong with it, if it seems a necessary part of some broader, bigger plan?" she said plaintively. "It would be a temporary thing, a curative thing, like a course of medicine."

Obaloluwa's voice rose. "Are you serious, Muonasa? There is nothing in the eyes of God, or in God's plan, that could demand or even approve of such behaviour. We know it is evil; it's as simple as that. Why is it that you do not seem able to hear me?" Muonasa said nothing but she placed her hand back in the pocket and held the stone.

After a few minutes, during which neither spoke or made eye contact, Obaloluwa frowned and looked at his sister. "Who has put these ideas in your head? Who did you see back home who advised you to do something so patently ludicrous?" and, again raising his voice, "Muonasa, tell me; I need to know!"

"Well, last time we spoke at least it was 'we' who needed to know. I am glad you are now being more honest that it is *you* who *needs* to know, as you put it."

Obaloluwa quietened and held her hand. Speaking gently, he said: "There are people in the world who are evil, who speak evil and who spread evil. They are out to destroy those whose mission in life is only good. I wish I did not have to say it but there are also those evil people back home - as there are everywhere."

Muonasa's other hand was now firmly wrapped around the stone which seemed, at least in her imagination, to be vibrating gently beneath her fingertips. She paused in her speaking, conscious of a gentle warmth moving up the palm of her hand into her forearm and then to her shoulder. *So satisfying; so comforting.* When she did start to speak, the sensation had spread to her lips, enveloping her mouth. In a way that she knew she would never be able to explain, the warmth even seemed to surround the words as they came out of her mouth.

"I want the best for you, Obaloluwa, and I am grateful for your caring and, I now realise, your constant love. You have been wonderful in the work you have done back home and, no doubt, here in England as well, although you haven't talked about that much. When you next return to Nigeria, even on a short visit, would it be possible for you to talk to the one who advised me? I am sure he would benefit from what you have to say and it may help you to understand the motives that lie behind my coming to this country - better than I could explain, I have no doubt. You do go back quite often, don't you?"

The stone moved again. "If it helps you, my sister, then I will," he said. "But I will also tell you this: Jesus Christ came onto this earth to eradicate evil and I have vowed to follow in his footsteps. It is bad enough to see the moral destruction in the whole world around me without also having to witness it in those closest to me - in my family - in my own sister!" His voice rose again. "Frankly, Muonasa, as your elder bother, I will not tolerate it! I will do anything - and I mean anything - to remove an evil curse upon my family. Do you understand?" His voice quietened and he cast his eyes downwards but he spoke with deliberation: "So now, Muonasa, the choice is yours: follow the path of this evil directive under the forsaken cloud of some bright vision ahead and experience the personal destruction to which it will lead or come to your senses, reject the sinful ways and live in God's protection to a truly wonderful future."

"So, will you meet my advisor and hear what he has to say?"

Obaloluwa sighed. "Yes, Muonasa, I will."

"When?"

"I will be back in Nigeria in two weeks. Tell me where to find him and I will see him."

"Thank you." Then, almost as an afterthought, she added: "And, by the way, I have some money to send him." The stone rumbled, then settled.

Obaloluwa returned to his office and got on with his work. Towards the end of the afternoon, when many of his colleagues had left and the department was quieter, he phoned Nigeria.

"How's it going? Good.....I'm fine but I have one or two problems at this end. My sister who is currently in London has been having dealings with some Yoruba guy. He has told her she has some illness or mental problem that can only be dealt with in London. I don't know the exact details and they don't really matter for our purposes. However, she has asked me to make contact with him when I am back home and wants me to take him some money that she has got."

"Well, you can probably see the difficulties already. I don't know yet who exactly he is but he lives in Oyo State, where we have been trying to set up the new churches, with some resistance from the Yoruba priests, as you know. There are too many connections building up for my liking. So far, we have managed to keep our operational details under wraps. However, if this guy manages to establish some connection between my sister, over whom he seems to have some control, me and our project, we may have problems. I will become the target of his resistance and, more importantly, he will then probe into our dealings in order to undermine us. It will not take him long to find out about our oil-selling project to the losers; the chief exec will find out and, not only will our jobs be on the line, but all our channeling of oil revenue to the church project will cease abruptly."

"Yes, yes, we could come clean and ask the chief exec to fund the churches in the open but we have talked about that before. We decided that he was unlikely to be sympathetic, not least because his family roots are deeply embedded in Yoruba tradition, even though he has moved on from there. Not only that but any money he is likely to give as a charitable donation would not come near what we are managing to cream off the company by what we are doing now. So we could never achieve as much for the Christian church as we can do now."

"What do you mean? Yes, 1 agree that the network of contact between my sister, the Yoruba guy and me has to be broken but how? I assume she still has contact with him but I confess I do not know for sure. But it seems likely. If I do not take the money to him, he will find out. And will find out who I am."

"I could refuse to take the money to him but the chances are that my sister will tell him what she has asked me to do; my name will come up and things will still unravel in the way I just described. All our plans will be thwarted."

"Yes, I agree that somehow we have to stop her talking to the Yoruba. Somehow. I'll think about it. In the meantime, make sure you get the cash for that latest shipment of oil as soon as possible. As always, get the money before the finer points of the shipment are gone through at the other side and get the paperwork sorted in advance with our friend in Legal. If there is any chance that our cover will be blown, we may as well get this deal tidied up first and lost into the morass with the others, not least because this is one of our bigger catches."

"Good, thanks. Let me know immediately if anyone comes asking questions, whether from the Yorubas or anyone else, and I'll work on somehow keeping my sister quiet."

"Would you like to go back to the graveyard?" asked Muonasa.

"Well, we can head out that way," said Adebanke, "maybe get some coffee again at Issa's. I'd rather not go back to the hotels today but we could go off the other way down to the park at the end. Why the graveyard anyway?"

"I think I told you; I just find them interesting."

Adebanke did not know then but, over the next few weeks, the graveyard would be a regular haunt of theirs on their days off together. The strong attachment that she felt for Muonasa - and the feeling was mutual - gave her the patience to be guided from headstone to headstone while her companion speculated, sometimes at length, on the likely cause of demise of the people interred there. After a few visits, Adebanke began to share the fascination and to feel some of the emotions that Muonasa experienced when focussing on the individuals within the graves. Yes, much of the basis for their feelings was speculative but that fact did not diminish the sense of bonding between them and the people who had once lived, whose bodies were in the ground beneath them and whose souls may be somewhere else.

On this occasion, to add a touch of variety to a routine limited in scope, they went to the graveyard before the coffee. Muonasa concentrated on a cluster of graves about ten yards from the path, away from the entrance to the church.

"This seems to be the area where the important people were buried," she said. "Perhaps they were the founders of this church. Yes, look, here is the first rector; he was head of this church but also, during his tenure, set up three satellite churches in villages nearby."

"How do you know that?" said Adebanke.

"Because it says so on his tombstone!"

"Well, at least this time you are basing your opinions on some evidence!"

"And, to his left, is the second rector and, to his right, the third." Wandering behind the three graves, she added, "And here are the rich men who paid for the buildings and gave the means necessary to spread the gospel message to the poor people, the folk who worked in the fields and needed persuasion to draw them from their insular, pastoral life into church, where they would receive guidance from God. How blessed are these men; may they all rest in peace!" She bowed her head and clasped her hands together.

"Nobody has disturbed them for four hundred years so, unless they build a motorway through the centre of London, it seems unlikely that anybody ever will," said Adebanke, smiling.

"I hope not," said Muonasa, "but, even if they do, their souls will still rest in peace."

"Do you think everyone believes that?"

"Probably not."

About twenty minutes later, they were settled at their usual table in the Egyptian coffee house. Issa brought their coffees without any need of asking and the girls engaged in the usual banter that they had discovered gave each a time of welcome relief from the other days. During a moment of laughter, Adebanke cast back her head and, with her right hand, brushed back her hair from her face to behind her right ear. Muonasa's smile ceased abruptly and, leaning forward, she gazed at an area between Adebanke's right eye and her cheekbone that had previously been hidden by the hair.

"What's that?" she cried.

"It's nothing," said her friend, pulling her hair forward again. "I caught it on my wardrobe door," and cast her eyes downwards.

"Oh no you didn't!" said Muonasa. "It's a burn - and, if I am not mistaken, it's pretty obviously a cigarette burn!" She placed her fingers gently on the skin next to it and added:

"And, since you do not smoke, I can only assume it was put there by someone else. Adebanke, where did you get it from?"

"Nowhere, it's nothing."

"And, Adebanke," said Muonasa looking more closely, "there's an oval red mark on your neck beneath your ear. Is that a pressure mark from someone's thumb?" Her voice rising in pitch and volume, she continued, "Has someone had their hands around your throat? Have they? Tell me, Adebanke!"

Adebanke raised her gaze and looked, with heavy eyes, into Muonasa's face.

"Well, it had to happen sometime, I guess. I suppose I am lucky that it hasn't happened before. Yes, I was sent out to a guy at one of the hotels and he gave me a rough time. A sick sadist - and I mean really sick. But somehow I sensed how to direct his perversions so I managed to get away with less than I might have done."

Muonasa moved her chair next to Adebanke's and put her arm around her shoulders. The two girls cried quietly together in silence. After several minutes, each of which seemed like an eternity to Muonasa, she said plaintively, "You won't have to go back to him again, will you? Adedayo said he would protect us."

"That doesn't apply to the hotels. As I said before, first of all he is not there but more important is that the hotel trade is controlled directly by the big guys - and they don't care too much what happens as long as they get their money. It will depend on how much the sick guy enjoyed it although there is also the possibility that he might not come back to these hotels. That might be my best chance."

It was a working day for Muonasa and, as was usual for her now, she dressed before breakfast. She and Adebanke had established a routine in which they would be ready for work before meeting in the kitchen and then eat breakfast standing together in the kitchen before each going their own way for the rest of the day. Muonasa was wearing the second outfit provided by Adedayo: white, three-quarter-sleeved, lace top with a crew neck; pleated, white, above-knee cotton skirt, white tights and low-heeled, white, matt leather shoes with a single strap. She descended the stairs , the impending brief rendezvous with her friend sufficient to sustain her in the hours to come.

But Adebanke was late. Even by the time Muonasa had prepared her porridge, she had not arrived. As Muonasa finished eating, so established was their morning pattern that she knew something was wrong. Adedayo arrived to tell her of her day's timetable even though both of them knew that this was only a broad plan because things could change at the last moment; someone would not turn up; another would arrive unappointed with an urgent request.

"Where is Adebanke?" said Muonasa.

"She didn't come home this morning.   It happens sometimes."

"Come home from where? From the hotels?"

"Yes.   As I said, it happens.   Sometimes they run away with one of the men; sometimes they want to get away - but that doesn't usually last long - and sometimes nobody ever knows what has happened."

"Adedayo, did you know she'd been attacked in one of the hotels? Did you send her back, knowing that?"

"I am not in control of what goes on in the hotels. I can look after you girls here but not everywhere. Your first client should be here in thirty minutes." And he left.

She went back to her room, turned to the stone and closed her eyes but no image appeared. She went through the day's work with more than her usual degree of abstraction. In the evening, as she put away her stone following a second fruitless visit to it that day, Adedayo appeared at her door.

"Adebanke has still not come back. Don't bother to ask me where she is; I don't know.   What I do know is that someone has to take her place. There is work to do at the hotels and the person to do that is you."

"But I am completely different from Adebanke," said Muonasa, with tangible desperation in her voice. "Her clients won't want the likes of me," she said, brushing her hands down the clothes that had been carefully chosen by Adedayo to convey an image.

"Well, as a matter of fact, Muonasa," said Adedayo, looking her up and down, "I wonder if they may not prefer you. Your image may appeal to their desires and, since you look so innocent, you may be less likely to get into trouble. So that's good news, eh?" and he smiled.

"So you admit that Adebanke 'got into trouble', as you call it. Why do you want to put me into the same vipers' den, the den of iniquity, the pit of destruction, the...the..the murderer's paradise?!"

"Fine words! But, as I keep telling you, I don't know what has happened to your friend. All I know is that my bosses have seen you two around and they think you would be good to take over from Adebanke in the hotels, wherever she is now. I understand that you know your way around - down the road from here, across the graveyard, down to the main road and you're practically there. But I will fill you in with the exact location and time when we get a booking. For now, goodnight!" He turned on his heel and left without waiting for a response.

As Muonasa took to her stone that evening, her heart grieved for her friend and the future that may be in store for her. She needed more than usual the comfort that came from the feel of the stone in her hands, the distant land to which it took her and the words of direction and succour from the voice and lately the face. As she held the stone as she always did across the fingertips of both hands, she took a deep breath and gazed downwards, ready to close her eyes. But she did not need to because there, on the surface of the stone in full vision with her eyes open, was the image of an elderly man with vertical scars down both cheeks, in full smile. Her counsellor, her director, her friend, her controller; yes, in one sighting, her mind flooded with the integrated but conflicting roles of her mentor. And that he was there in real life - not literally perhaps, but almost, for no longer could she tell herself that he was a product of her memory, her imagination, her own cognitive reinforcement of a message, yes Adebanke, even a spell, imparted to her in a town in Nigeria many weeks ago. Because there, with her eyes open, in full consciousness, she was seeing him in her room, in her presence, in her being. And it wasn't just an image because he was animate; his lips were moving and she could hear his voice. She closed her eyes and opened them again but he was still there. She closed her eyes for longer but she still heard his voice. She opened them again and listened.

"Muonasa, now is not the time to feel fear. Now is the time to galvanise yourself to action. You have lost a dear friend but there is purpose in everything, however difficult it may seem to appreciate or understand it. You set yourself on a road to freedom; now you are about to leave the minor pathways and embark on the main thoroughfare to your goal. From the outset, you knew I would always be with you, to send you in the appropriate direction, support you along the way and ensure that you continued on the right route to your goal. Nothing has changed and, to prove it, here I am, just as I was on that day when you discovered that I had the means to procure your release - release from the illness, the bad spirits and the thoughts that surrounded them. Carry on, Muonasa; the frail human mind is so often inadequate to understand the complex powers that supersede the simple processes of this world. But trust me because I do understand."

She closed her eyes again. The voice gradually drifted away until it lost first its volume and then its intelligibility. When she opened her eyes, the face had gone. After putting back the stone, she stood, walked to the window and looked out. She saw no sign of a man in a hoodie, an emaciated tragic figure, a body staggering or lying by the roadside or a black BMW. Relieved, she sighed deeply, felt a sense of determination, got undressed and retired to bed. She did not know yet what the next few days would bring but she did know that tomorrow she would be seeing Mark Haynes.

Adedayo was sitting in his room, head back, eyes closed, puffing on his pipe. His body was relaxed and his mind was floating. *No fear, not now, maybe never. This is my moment. The world can go away, leave me here and I will be happy.* But then there came a rapping on the front door of the house, shaking his dream in a flash. He came back to consciousness with a start.

None of the regulars are booked in and this is not the time for the arrival of our casual visitors. Who the hell is it?

He scurried to the door and dragged it open in obvious irritation. He scowled at the face of the visitor whom he did not recognise. "Yes?!" he said.

"Don't you remember me?" said Obaloluwa.

"No, I'm afraid I don't," said Adedayo with an air of disinterest.

"Well, let me remind you. A little while ago, you delivered a letter from me to my sister, who is living in your house."

"OK, so what?"

"I'll tell you what," said Obaloluwa, raising his voice. "As I said, she is my sister and her welfare is my primary concern. I want to know what you are doing with her in this place of yours. I want to know what *exactly* you are doing with her in this place of yours."

"Well, I think you know already - she is a resident and I am her landlord."

"And?" said Obaloluwa.

"And what?" said Adedayo.

"And you know what else," said Obaloluwa, in increasing agitation. "Look - let's not beat around the bush - I know what goes on here and I don't like the idea that my sister may be involved in it. In fact, I don't like it very much at all."

"This is a residential house and your sister is a member of it. I don't know what else you are talking about."

"Well, that's very convenient amnesia," said Obaloluwa. Then, grabbing Adedayo by the lapels of his jacket and beginning to shout, he continued, "I, and probably everyone else who has eyes to see, knows that this place is a brothel - and you, my friend, are its pimp. I have come here in the probably forlorn hope that you might be able to convince me that my sister is somehow different, that she is not, like the other poor losers you have here, involved in your vile trade. Because - and this you may find difficult to understand - it matters to me. And, I will tell you, it matters to powers that are way beyond your understanding!"

"What your sister does is up to her."

"And you have nothing to do with it? If you expect me to believe that, you underestimate me, my friend."

"I am sorry," said Adedayo, "but I am busy. I am not answerable to you and, dare I suggest it, neither is your sister. If you want to know what she is doing, I suggest you speak to her but I cannot speak on her behalf. Now I have to go."

"Well, that is where you are wrong!" said Obaloluwa, now shouting. "You - and she - are answerable to me because I have decided that you are! I am not going to allow her to behave like a slut. I - and my family - simply will not tolerate it. Again you probably would not understand but we live our life by the rule of God and what she is doing, with your support, is totally unacceptable. We will stop it, clean it out of our family, by whatever means are necessary. A life of sin leads only to death. Do you understand me?"

"I have to go," said Adedayo. "Goodbye." Although Obaloluwa tried to jam his foot in the way of the closing door, Adedayo lent his weight against it and slammed it in Obaloluwa's face.

"You - and she - will regret that," mumbled Obaloluwa, as he turned and sloped away.

As Muonasa set off to the hotel quarter that evening, her mind rekindled the memories of that first day's work in the house: the lack of knowledge of exactly what was to come, the trepidation, the faint sense of disgust. By now, she had become accustomed to that routine and, although a part of her retained that revulsion, the confidence that she was pursuing a necessary mission, nurtured by her regular contact with the stone, maintained her. But her new task was different; not only was there a change of surroundings that deprived her of the comfort of familiarity but the belief that Adedayo provided a background safety net, however misplaced and unrealistic that belief may have been in practice, was now absent; and, finally, she was about to enter territory that may have taken away one of the few pillars that supported her in her quest, Adebanke. But, she reminded herself, she still had the stone, the priest, if he would see her again, and, of course, Mark Haynes.

She trod the route with heavy steps: down to the end of the road, right to a T-junction, then left and through a gate to the path across the churchyard. She paused for a few minutes to re-examine the headstones that had previously occupied Adebanke and her. She stood in silence for several minutes, eyes closed, at the grave of the first rector and said a prayer, initially for the souls of those who had worked to establish the church in that area, then for her brother, for her family and community back home, for Adebanke and finally for herself. She renewed her promise to God that nothing, despite the seeming incongruity of her present situation, would turn her away from Him and, in that, she gained another support for her to carry on, a support that she realised she had perhaps forgotten for a while. With renewed vigour, she passed through the gate at the far end of the graveyard, turned left and headed towards the hotels.

As instructed, she called at the reception desk for an envelope addressed to her, took out the room key and headed upstairs to room 531. She paused at the door for a minute or so before placing the card in the slot in the door, waiting for the green light and then opening the door.

She was in a hurry to return to the house the following morning, anxious to take a bath, change her clothes and somehow recover. She walked almost at a trotting pace but, again in the graveyard, felt the need to loiter for a while. She wandered among the three or four main graves in the area closest to the church, as she had done with Adebanke. The same thoughts recurred: here was the foundation of Christianity in the area; here lay the souls of those who had worked for it yet, despite all that, evil flourished and even she, who had thought she was close to the faith, had taken another path in an attempt to gain easy happiness. *So easy, it is,* she thought, *to take the easy route and how difficult to take the one that will ultimately work.*

When she entered the house, she found Adedayo counting a small wadge of banknotes in the hall. Apart from a cursory nod, he was about to ignore her but Muonasa was too emotionally charged to let pass the opportunity to try to make him understand how she might be feeling. She began speaking but he waved her down until he had finished counting, made a note on a scrap of paper and turned towards her. He indicated his willingness to listen by looking into her eyes, raising an eyebrow and showing a touch of a smile.

"Adedayo, I cannot go on doing this; you've got to help me. The business in the house was bad enough but at least the men that you chose for me were fairly, well to some extent, considerate. This new stuff is on a different level. That guy last night is verging on psychotic. Have you any idea what he's like? Was it the same one that you sent Adebanke to?"

"It's all part of the business, Muonasa. Sometimes we have to take the rough with the smooth."

"I assume you did not intend that to be a pun but, if so, it's not very funny!"

"Muonasa, we have no choice. Sometimes I think I wish I were doing something different but I can't. Go back to your room, get some sleep, freshen up and take the rest of the day off. We have no more work for you today."

"Why do you have no choice?"

"Don't ask, Muonasa; don't ask."

For the first time, she felt reluctance to turn to the stone. Despite questioning herself, she could not understand why, when it had always been her point of reference in a world of chaos. But she did and again the face appeared before she closed her eyes.

"*I know what you are thinking, Muonasa, and it is not good. The thoughts you are having are destructive, destructive to our plan. You must not let them flourish for they can only lead you to misery. Nothing that is worth having is acquired easily; you need to work to achieve your dreams, your release, your cleansing. Why do rainbows only appear after rain? Why do flowers only bloom in the dirty earth? Why is light most powerful when it enters darkness? Heed my advice, Muonasa, and stay on the path that has been laid out for you. Sometimes the most wonderful things come from places that we least understand. I assure you that, if you let these present thoughts develop, you will only be led to catastrophe.*"

Muonasa's second visit to the hotel area was a replica of the first but more intense. On this occasion, apart from psychological trauma, her experience had gained her bruises to both upper arms, inflicted by two strong grips, a knee-shaped bruise on her left inner thigh and the loss of some hair. She ran down the stairs without waiting for the lift, stumbled out of the hotel, her concentration clouded by a flood of mixed emotions, and walked slowly down the road towards the graveyard. Her stay there was longer than previously as she spent time sitting on one of the gravestones in quiet refection and prayer.

By the time she reached the house, her reaction to the experience was entrenched. She ran up to her room but Adedayo had heard her enter and followed her upstairs. As he opened the door, he saw her lying on the bed, staring up at the ceiling. Although he had expected to find her crying, she was quiet and her body motionless, apart from deep breathing.

"I cannot do any more," she said quietly, in measured tone.

"He may not need you again," said Adedayo. "We know he is staying again next week but nothing is booked yet. So that might be your last time."

"And it might not," she said. "But, if I have anything to do with it, it will be."

"You know you cannot say that, Muonasa. This is the life that has been laid out for us. There are people watching us and they know every step we take."

A few days later, the call did indeed come again and, at nine p.m., Adedayo appeared at her door and told her to get herself ready and be at the hotel for ten p.m. For the next twenty minutes, she sat on the edge of the bed, head bowed. Not much of substance passed through her thoughts because she had rationalised the likelihood of this moment after her last visit and had already anticipated the depths of dread consequent upon it. But what she did think was that she did not have to do it; she did have a choice, however difficult the outcome to which a choice against may lead and it was that realisation that occupied most of her thinking time.

As she looked up, she caught sight of her stone on the bedside table, reached out but then drew back. If I am going to be strong enough to beat this, she thought, I will have to do it on my own. A lucky stone, perhaps, but surely nothing could be lucky enough to help me in what I have to do now. I will go to the graveyard and take my strength from those souls who have hitherto shown far more fortitude and determination in their mission than I am required to do now. She stood up and turned away from the table to put on her shoes. As she reached down to the floor to pick them up, she heard a voice from behind.

Muonasa!

Thinking Adedayo had re-entered, she turned around and saw flickering movements on the surface of the stone. Approaching closer, she could see the familiar image of her mentor and guardian, upon whom she had relied for support until the declaration of self-intent made to herself a few minutes earlier. She looked into the stone.

Muonasa, you have let yourself be controlled by your evil spirit of which we are trying to rid you. It will only cause you harm. Do you remember your lack of self worth that you felt and displayed to me when we first met? How your family and community had instilled within you all your negative feelings? I showed you the presence of the spirit that was the cause of these emotions and implanted within you a good spirit that would fight and destroy the evil one, provided you followed its directions. But you are not doing that, Muonasa; you have let the Bad One rise up and give you false hopes. A straight path may be long with side roads along the way but, even though you are tired, you need to stay on the straight path if you want to get to your destination. The side roads may lead to cosy glades of trees and water, where you can rest, refresh yourself and feel at ease but, if you want to reach your final resting place, you would have to go back up the side roads and join the main path again. In the end, you will have travelled further. Follow the plan. I will stay with you along the way, as I have done since the day we met. Now dress yourself for the next step and go out to do what is necessary to move along the path. And remember, take me with you so that I can support you every minute of your journey. That way, we will see it through together. But remember, if you do not, the side road you take may lead you to a bog, a quagmire, from which you cannot escape. And never will.

Renewed with some positivity, she changed into her hot pants, T-shirt and ballet pumps, took the stone in her right hand and left the house. But the desire to speak with her new friends, the lost Christian souls, had not left her. And she knew that it never would.

Adedayo walked briskly back home, through the graveyard, with a racing mind. Closing his front door behind him, he stopped in the hall, breathing purposefully, before entering his ground-floor room, reaching into a low cupboard and taking out a glass pipe, a flame lighter and a small packet of white crystals. He loaded the crystals into the pipe, struck the lighter and applied the flame to the base of the pipe. When the crystals were melting, he took several puffs and began to feel the rush as his heart raced. After a couple of minutes, he began to experience the familiar high. But then his mind focussed on the girl Muonasa, to the exclusion of almost everything else. He just managed to take the pipe from his mouth and put it on the bedside table. *Later*, he thought, and put the rest of the paraphernalia next to the pipe.

Then thoughts rushed through his mind, one after another in close succession. *Let's check, let's check! As instructed, I have destroyed the leather pouch by her bedside; and I have moved the stone from the side of the body and hidden it where they told me. Yes, put it there and they will pick it up and move it into its resting place. Is that what they meant?*

I hope so, I really hope so. I had such little time when those cops were distracted; it could so easily have gone wrong and, as usual, it would have been me that was in the line of fire, not them. Oh well, now I have to check that her bedroom is as she left it except to remove any other so-called "important items". Like what, I wonder? Why move the stone anyway? And where are they moving it to? And why? Why not just destroy it, like the pouch? Or leave it where it is? Come on, Adedayo! At least you are doing what you are told and are being paid for it. Let's just do it! Calm down, for goodness sake! The job's nearly done!

Then his agitation began to settle. The focus of his mind seemed to spread so that he became aware of other thoughts creeping into the centre of his attention, as if from its periphery. *Did I do all that? I know that was the laid-out plan but did I do it? Who told me to do it anyway? I can't remember right now. Have I just dreamt everything? Was that really the plan? Did it happen? Need to relax.*

He went up to her bedroom and scanned the contents from the door. The hot pants and T-shirt lying on the floor he hung in the wardrobe at the far left and pushed the hangers holding her non-working clothes against them so they would not be seen by a casual observer. He checked the drawers and moved her lace underwear underneath the less flamboyant cotton items. Nothing much else needed attention. *Well, at least Muonasa was tidy and thank goodness for that*, he thought.

Adedayo closed and locked the door, returned to his own room and retrieved the pipe, lighter and crystals. *Tomorrow is another day.*

Chapter 9

"Well, boss, your suspicions were right," said Detective Sergeant Lees as he walked into the office. "It certainly is an odd business. The scene of crime boys have not quite finished sussing out the place but already they've thrown out a number of questions. Not easy ones either. I think we are going to be busy as, I might add, are forensics."

"Tell me the gist of it," said Detective Inspector Griffiths, putting down the social report he had just removed from its envelope and lifting up his coffee cup.

"It's lucky we have a stomach for these things," said DS Lees and took a deep breath. "A body has been found, face down, in the graveyard. We assume it's a human body from the shape of it but you would not otherwise know because it is virtually entirely destroyed. The body has obviously been on fire because it is reduced almost to ash. The conclusion that it is a human body comes from the form - the shape - formed by the ash. So it lies roughly in a pattern that you can recognise as a head, body, two arms and two legs. And the ash lies in piles that give some three-dimensional aspects to the shapes, adding evidence that it is - or was - a human body. In other words, boss, it is a load of ash in the shape of a human body."

"When was it found?"

"About six o'clock this morning by someone walking through the graveyard," said the DS. "As you know, that is a route taken by many people heading between home and the shops and hotels where they work. The body was found by a twenty-year-old Polish girl who had just finished the night shift at one of the hotels and was heading back home. Luckily

- for us, that is - she used the same short cut on her way to work at about 9:45 the previous evening and was certain that there was nothing wrong then. You might ask whether she could be sure because it was dark then, unlike this morning. However, apparently she always uses a torch and flashes it regularly from side to side because she finds the graveyard a bit eerie. But the route is convenient, which is why she uses it."

"Anyway, assuming she is right, that puts the time of death to between about ten o'clock last night and six this morning."

"Was there any sign of continuing combustion," asked the inspector, "that might help put the time nearer six a.m. than ten p.m.?"

"None whatsoever," replied the sergeant. "Any fire was well and truly out by then. There was not even any warmth coming from the ash. And that's another odd thing - the scene of crime guys seem to think that a fire of that intensity would probably still show at least some warmth even if it had started at ten o'clock last night. But they admit they are not experts and said we should ask forensics. Intriguing though, eh?"

"Well, it is," admitted the inspector. "How did the fire start?" he added. "Do we know? Was there any sign of anything around that could have been used to start the fire?"

"No, nothing. The only things found at the scene, apart from the ash, were a necklace and a stone."

"A stone? So what?"

"No, not just an ordinary stone. Apparently, it had been decorated. Some sort of ornament, I guess. The scene of crime boys have taken some photos of the two objects because obviously they might give a clue to the identity of the body.

But no idea so far. Oh, by the way, that's not all." He paused and smiled, waiting for his superior's inquisitiveness to mount.

"What else?" demanded the DI.

"There is practically no sign of fire damage outside of the body. Despite the body lying on grass, not a blade of it appears to be scorched. And no fire or smoke damage to the neighbouring gravestones. How about that?"

"Impossible," said the inspector, "unless the grass was wet."

"Which it wasn't," said the sergeant. "It was a dry night."

"Go and find some more evidence!" The inspector terminated a discussion that he was beginning to find frustrating and frankly fanciful. Too much imagination, that DS, he thought. Why does he put forward observations that he must know are inaccurate because they are plainly illogical? Is he going to have to do the leg work on every case himself? Well, maybe in the end it would be quicker, he pondered, because then he would not have to waste precious time in listening to irrelevancies.

He returned to the report. Criminal Justice Social Work - now there's another pointless profession. A set of do-gooders trying to handcuff the arms of justice by claiming that no criminal is responsible for their actions and that society, in some form or another, is really to blame. Well, that may be an exaggeration, one half of his brain acknowledged to the other, but sometimes it's not far from the truth.

What's this one about? Oh, yes, it concerns that hooker who was picked up going back home, if that's what you can call it, after a night at a hotel, looking the worse for wear. The concierge took exception to her leaving the hotel in the early hours of the morning, was concerned about bruises around her face, suspected she was a prostitute and called the police. The uniformed guys had to do their duty and took her in for investigation on suspicion that she was operating from a brothel and may have been subject to violence. Unfortunately, she denied all those claims and didn't want to press charges. She admitted being a prostitute but, as she pointed out, that in itself is not illegal.

How on earth did the social workers get involved? Some caring person in the station, no doubt. Quite what they will have concluded, beyond what we already know, will be interesting. Hope it's more than that there is a Nigerian pimp house near the hotels that regularly supplies services to its customers and that some of the clients have rather specialist tastes in that department.

He flicked over the pages to the summary of conclusions.

Well, surprise, surprise! There are several *mostly Nigerian brothels in the area which, among other activities, supply prostitutes to hotels nearby, etcetera, etcetera. Extreme noises heard coming from the establishments....girls may be victims of trafficking....mostly poor and uneducated....*

Oh, this is a new one but hardly surprising: Hotel managers are beginning to be concerned about the expanding trade in prostitution on their premises for fear that it will deter other customers and "lower the tone of the area". Bit late, I'd say.

"In interview, some hotel managers and owners of smaller establishments were forthright in their views on this trade, even to the point of vitriol. In addition, in the opinions of the interviewers, there was likely to be a strong racist component to their objections." *Now that is interesting,* thought DI

Griffiths and cast his mind back to the burnt body in the graveyard.

The sergeant left his inspector to his thoughts. The DI tried to refocus on the report but failed.

I'd better go and look myself, he thought, threw the report onto his desk, snatched his coat from the rack and marched out the door. He needed his sergeant with him but fortunately he had not got very far before the DI found him in the anteroom gulping down a quick coffee before he set out to find further evidence. *Though that may be wishful thinking*, thought the DS.

"Come with me!" barked the DI.

At the churchyard, DS Lees began his description of the scene in a fashion true to his training but his boss cut him short because everything he had to say was laid out before them. Steve Griffiths walked around the charred mass on the ground with his subordinate following a respectful distance behind the DI's right shoulder.

"Well, so far it seems you are right, Detective Sergeant," said the DI. "We have a mass of virtually destroyed - material, should I call it? A pile of ash that conforms to the shape of a body. But nothing else would lead you to conclude that it was once human - except that necklace," he said, pointing towards the upper part of the body, "but that's circumstantial at best."

Bending forwards to examine it better, he continued, "Well, there is some fire damage but you can still see its basic design. Quite elaborate, isn't it? And that metal must be fairly robust to have withstood the fire so well. It certainly would help to know the origin of jewellery like that."

"Sure," said Lees, 'but the truth is there are lots of places in London that sell all kinds of fancy jewellery so it may not help that much." Reluctantly, Griffiths agreed.

The DI was about to move off but then stopped suddenly. "Where's this stone that you mentioned?"

"It was said to be just by the body. Er, hang on, it must be somewhere," said Lees, starting to walk rapidly up and down the line of the body. "I can't see it, boss. Where the hell is it?"

"It was definitely near the body, was it?" said the DI.

"Yes, according to the report - just by the side - as if it had been in her hand."

"Sure, that's what I thought - just checking. And I'm assuming scene of crime did not remove it?"

"Definitely not. They photographed it - that's all."

"We'll look at the pics later. Right now, let's go and have a word with the uniforms."

The uniformed officers confirmed that at least one member of their force had been present at the scene since they were first alerted and they were not aware of anyone having removed the stone or even acting suspiciously. Reluctantly, the detectives had to leave it at that and decided to look for any other evidence. They set off back to the body.

The DI cast his eyes sideways as he continued to walk around the scene.

"And, yes, there is no sign of burning to any of the grass around it. How can that be?"

He stopped, raised his head upwards and held out his hands in front of him.

"Could this be some sort of joke? Could someone just have gathered together the contents of their garden burner - or whatever - and placed it here to entice the likes of you and me? Pretty sick, if so - and frankly irritating. If that's what it is, we will send them up for wasting police time!"

"Well, maybe not," said the DS, looking at the ash. "Is that a piece of bone sticking out from the rest?"

Griffiths turned and bent low at the waist to stare at where the DS was pointing.

"Could be, Lees; could be." Then standing straight again, and turning to his DS, he added, "Forensics can sort it out." He began to walk off but paused and turned back. "I do agree, however, that that is important and thank you, Lees, for pointing it out. Let's go and look at the rest of the place."

As they walked around the graveyard, DI Griffiths was deep in thought. His sergeant knew him well enough not to disturb him on such occasions unless it was absolutely necessary but, after several minutes, he could not resist.

"Boss, you thought all this might be some kind of sick joke. Well, I was just thinking that it would take quite a lot of effort to transport the ash - what is basically powder - and arrange it in such a perfect form of a body. That would take some time and someone might well have seen them doing it. Not only that - surely he - or she - would have spilt some of the ash around the place while they were constructing their artwork but there is no ash anywhere else. If they did do that, they must have done it really quickly and with great skill."

"You might be right, Lees; you might be right."

"So, assuming this is indeed a burnt body," continued the inspector, "let's leave aside for a moment exactly how it happened and see if we can find out who it is and who might have done it. The latter might depend quite heavily on finding out who was the victim. Check through the missing persons file, new registrants to the area, anyone who has a history of this sort of crime - the usual - but maybe focus on trying to find out the identity of this pile of ash." He sighed and shook his head in some desperation and walked on. "Oh, and by the way, get those photos of the stone PDQ - and preferably find out what has happened to it."

Two days later, the inspector walked into his office to find an open A4 envelope on his desk. He pulled out the contents and spread out the photographs between his table lamp and an empty coffee cup. Just as he had finished studying each one in detail, his sergeant came in.

"Have you seen these pictures?" asked Griffiths.

"Yes, they arrived this morning. I put them on your desk."

"And what do you make of them?"

"Interesting, I'd say."

"Could you be more precise?"

The sergeant explained that he was no expert in jewellery or decorative objects but he could pass on the observations of the research team, who sadly had not concluded very much. The necklace was fairly flamboyant by most British tastes and could broadly be described as ethnic. However, jewellery like that could be obtained in many shops in London (a finding at which the DS could not conceal his joy, because, after all, he had thought of that first). It was also popular amongst younger women, which gave perhaps a small clue to the identity of the victim.

"So it's likely to be female?" said Griffiths.

"Sadly, not necessarily, " said the sergeant, "because, as I'm sure you know, some young men are also prone to wearing strange things. But I suppose it's more likely than not."

"And the stone?"

Lees said that the team had been even less helpful there except to confirm that no-one from uniform, scene of crime or anyone else in the force had removed it. So its whereabouts was still a mystery. As for the stone itself, the photos suggest simply that it is a smooth, oval stone decorated around the edge with small heads. The one thing they did say, he added, was that the heads look to be non-whites - African, Asian or native Australian, for example.

"Which I suppose is helpful?" said Griffiths.

"Yes, but again sadly there are many places in London that sell decorative objects similar to that - well, in principle, at any rate."

"But why would she - or he - carry it about with them?"

"No idea. For sentimental reasons, maybe?"

"We've got the forensics report!" shouted DI Griffiths as his sergeant walked into the office, coffee cup in hand. "And very interesting reading it makes too."

"Great stuff!" said the DS. "Does it tell us who has died, how it was done and, if it was murder, who did it?!"

"This is no time for jokes, Sergeant," said Griffiths.

"Sorry, boss, but forensics are always telling us that they are the ones who provide the key bits of evidence so I like to marvel at what they will come up with next!"

"Well, that much is true," said the DI, smiling. "But actually, on this occasion, they seem to have done quite a good job."

"What have they found?"

"You were right, Lees - that bit sticking up from the ash was a piece of bone and there was enough DNA left in it for them to do a pretty decent analysis. They have concluded, with ninety percent confidence, that the victim was female. Oh, before that, I suppose I had better point out that the burnt tissue was human. I guess that's pretty obvious but, in this situation, who knows? Anyway, it was very likely a female human. Not only that - and this is where they have come into their own - she was probably African - eighty percent certain - and likely from West Africa, somewhere like Nigeria - sixty-five percent certain."

"Wow!" said Lees. "That is what I call useful."

"That's what I call useful too," said the DI.

"Any thoughts on the manner of death?" asked Lees.

"There they were less helpful except to add to the mystery. In fact, you might think they were overstepping their mark because they seem to have ended up as speculative as we are. Maybe we need a pyrotechnics expert."

"A what?"

"A pyrotechnics expert - someone who knows about fires. Well, not as simple as that - about how they start, what happens with a particular kind of fire, how fast they start and cool off - that kind of thing."

"Anyway, what did forensics say?"

"They said that the extent of destruction of the body would have required a very intense heat, especially since it all seemed to occur over a few hours, at least as judged by the timings that we have so far. Like all of us, they considered two possibilities: suicide and murder. They left it to us to decide, if it was murder, whether the person was killed at the scene or had been brought dead to the graveyard and then set alight.

From their point of view, it didn't make much difference - in terms of the way the body was destroyed."

"But the postmortem changes would be more profound if they were dead when they were brought there, wouldn't they?" said Lees.

"Yes, but all of that went up in smoke. Any postmortem changes would have been destroyed in the fire."

"OK."

"What they did say was that someone committing suicide would have had to have brought a lot of materials to produce a fire of that intensity. It is possible that all that was destroyed in the fire but suiciders are not usually that careful; forensics would have expected that at least something - fuel container, box of matches, a bag, for example - would have been discarded outside of the scene of the fire. Especially, they add, since the fire seems to have been contained within a very defined area."

"So it was murder?"

"Well, so far, that seems more likely of the two. The perpetrator would have been careful to remove all evidence from the scene, obviously to avoid incrimination. If the victim was killed before being brought to the graveyard, we don't even have to expect evidence of the means of death at the scene. We'd have to look elsewhere for that."

"OK, so we have a West-African lady who has been murdered and set alight in a graveyard? That sounds workable."

"Not entirely, I am afraid, because forensics have raised a third possibility - over and above the two we have, suicide and murder."

"And what's that?"

"Spontaneous combustion."

"I'm no wiser. What the hell is that?"

"Apparently, what puzzles forensics is that the fire must have been intense, as I've said. But, like us, they examined the area around and found no sign of burning. They even took samples of the grass to look for signs of charcoal deposition or oxidation - in other words, signs of heat damage - and found none. That is not what you would expect with a normal fire, especially one of intensity."

"So?"

"They say that there have been reports over the years concerning bodies that seem to have ignited spontaneously, on their own, without something or someone actually setting fire to them. And, in those cases - they say - there was no damage to the areas around the body. If you ask me, believe that and you will believe anything. But that's what they say."

"And, as we know, they are the experts!"

"Quite so."

"So where do we go now?"

"What I think is hard evidence from this report is that the victim was probably a West-African, maybe Nigerian, female. Let's start looking for someone of that description who has gone missing. Especially someone who might disappear without too many people raising a fuss. I do not want to be presumptuous but you might start in one of the brothels nearby that specialises in women of Nigerian extract."

"I'll get on to it right away."

"Thanks. What I'll do is to get back to forensics about this spontaneous human combustion bit and ask them to research it in more detail. It seems so far fetched that we cannot take it on board as a possibility unless we have a lot more evidence.

If we can rule that out as just a fanciful idea, we can focus on the only other likely possibility - murder - and then do our normal detective work to nail the culprit."

"OK. See you later."

Chapter 10

My dear Sarah,

Thank you so much for your latest letter. I was delighted to hear of your new appointment in the Faculty. Your career has always been a bit of a mystery to me and I confess I do not fully understand the difference between African Culture and African Social Anthropology but I assume it is because they are related that you were able to move from one department to another! Anyway, it sounds like a positive move so I am very happy for you.

I appreciate that you think your ideas may be tangential and possibly irrelevant but they are helpful nonetheless. Indeed, any thoughts on this mystery would be welcome but especially ones coming from someone as informed as you are.

No, I do not know whether the stone is important or not, far less why and how it moved from the original site of the death. If indeed the victim is one of the Nigerian girls who have gone missing from the brothel houses in the area, then your ideas could be more relevant than you imagine. I will certainly bring them to the attention of Inspector Griffiths.

You have provided a lot of detail - and again thank you. But I want to be sure that I have understood the essence of it. To summarise the details you provided, it seems there are two viable reasons why a decorated stone could be associated with a Nigerian girl, if, as I have said, such a person is the victim. First, if she stems from the Yoruba tribe, and is a devotee of the Yoruba religion, the stone may represent a tangible representation of a god - although not all members of that religion subscribe to that view so there is a caveat there already. Secondly, and I understand this may be even more conjectural, there is an old Nigerian folk tale about a magic stone, which might suggest that she kept the stone as some kind of good luck charm. You cannot think of any other significance to the decorated stone. Please correct me if I have misunderstood the points you raised.

Sadly, even if you are correct, I cannot imagine any association between either of your two observations and a reason for suicide or murder but maybe the detectives, with their experience, will think of one. Do not let this comment put you off; if you think of any other evidence that could even conceivably be relevant, do let me know for you are an expert and we are short of leads.

Once again, thank you - and congratulations again! I hope your new position provides everything that you had hoped for.

Much love,

Julian

Let's see, thought Detective Inspector Steve Griffiths, as he thumbed through the sheaf of articles that had arrived on his desk. His eyes settled on one which he separated from the rest.

Spontaneous human combustion - "A term used since 1746, although cases were reported before, perhaps as early as the fifteenth century. Perhaps two hundred cases in total".

He read on. He discovered that, in 1725, Nicole Millet, the wife of a Parisian innkeeper, was found in the kitchen with her body reduced virtually to ash but the wooden utensils around her were intact. Some reports say that she burned on a straw pallet, which was also virtually undamaged. Her husband was found guilty of murder but was cleared on appeal by a defence of "spontaneous human combustion". The cause was put down to a visitation from God.

In 1951, in St. Petersburg, Florida, Mary Hardy Reeser was found, reduced to ash by fire, except for a skull and a completely undamaged foot, clad in an intact satin slipper. The carpet was scorched but a nearby chair, table and pile of newspapers were untouched by the flames.

In the 1970s, Ginette Kazmierczak's husband disappeared and could not be found. Several days later, Ginette's body was found reduced to ash, except for her legs, in an apartment that was otherwise undisturbed.

One case of spontaneous human combustion has been witnessed. In 1982, a father saw a flash and turned his head to see his mentally disabled daughter, Jeannie Saffin, on fire. She appeared to be unconcerned as to what was happening. She lived through the fire but remained in a coma and died soon after.

Even Dickens recorded spontaneous human combustion in his book, Bleak House.

DI Griffiths skipped the rest of the cases described. He felt he had got the gist. His eyes scanned further down the article.

Characteristics - "No fire damage to surrounding objects".

Well, that would fit, he thought, *although the body was lying on grass which does not catch fire that easily at the best of times and was a bit damp, at the time that she was found, at least.*

"A residue of nasty-smelling grease and ashes". *Well, I suppose so but no more than any other burnt body I have seen - which, thinking about it, I guess is not that many.*

"Limbs often fall off." *No idea - they had gone up in smoke as well .*

"Often elderly female alcoholics." *Can't be sure. None of the people on the current missing persons list is an elderly female. Nor alcoholic. And the number of our friends living on the street in the area does not seem recognisably reduced. I'll say one thing for that lot - they look after each other as far as they can and they know what's going on in their community. They would know if one had disappeared and I can see no reason why they would not have told the PCs when they asked around.*

But someone from outside? Who knows? But then why would they come here? These boozers don't tend to travel far.

And that latest report of the girl missing from the Nigerian pimp house. Well, we can be sure she wasn't elderly and probably not alcoholic either - at least not if she planned to make much money from the trade, his mind added as an afterthought. Steve Griffiths sniggered to himself in appreciation of his own joke.

He read on: "Stevens-Johnson syndrome is a medical condition that can cause burn-like blisters and may be fatal. The corpse may resemble a partially burnt body." *Not here,* thought Steve; *her body was virtually reduced to ash.* "The existence of the phenomenon is disputed, some authors suggesting that, in most cases, the bodies lay close to some plausible ignition source." *Not spontaneous then,* thought the detective. *But definitely not applicable in this case. The guys first on the scene, the scene-of-crime boys and forensics all agree that there was definitely nothing in the area that could have ignited the body, either accidentally or deliberately.*

But can we be sure? Could she have committed suicide by setting fire to herself and the means of her doing so have been lost in the flames? Supposing she had petrol in a plastic bag and a wooden match - they would all have been burnt up in the fire. Oh, I don't know. Why not just leave it to forensics? It's their job after all. I guess they have copies of these articles - and hopefully more besides.

DI Griffiths decided to concentrate on what he was good at and made himself a cup of coffee. *Still, can't wait to see what forensics come up with,* he thought.

"Well, your hunch might well have been correct," said DS Lees. "I've been down the road that we all know well - not from personal experience, I might add - and knocked on a few doors. I got to speak to this guy at one of the places who opened the door with a pipe in his hand. I don't think it contained tobacco but we'll let that pass for the moment. We can always use it later if he refuses to cooperate."

"Get to the point, Lees," said the DI.

"To be fair, he did cooperate quite well. At least, he answered my questions which, judging by the state he was in, was pretty remarkable in itself. Maybe something to do with the pipe!"

"Lees, I said get to the point!"

"Well, it seems there are a number of Nigerians living in the house. He was at pains to point out that it was a residential home where visitors to the country rent a room and he did not routinely enquire about the nature of their employment because it was not necessary as long as they paid their rent. But strangely all the occupants are women; don't you think that's an odd coincidence?" He laughed.

"Lees, I have been grappling - once again - with this social work report for the last hour and I am in no mood for your jokes, sarcasm or whatever you like to call it. I beg you, please get to the point."

"OK, fair enough. Well, it turns out that not one but *two* women have recently left the house without giving notice, one a few weeks ago and the second - wait for it - a few days ago. She did not come back at the end of the day, which he thought was odd because previously she had done so without fail. But he wasn't too concerned because obviously, he said, her life was her own and why shouldn't she go away for a few nights? Yeh, right!"

"And what about the first?" asked Griffiths.

"He doesn't know. She just left."

"And, don't tell me, he wasn't concerned, or thought of telling the police, because she was up to date with her rent, her life was her own and she could do what she wants."

"Bang on!" said Lees. "You could be a detective!"

"And did either of these girls take any of their belongings with them?"

"Not as far as he can see," said Lees, "but he hasn't looked through the second girl's things in detail because she has not been gone long and it would be impolite. Can you believe this?"

169

"But he doesn't think it odd that the first girl would simply leave, apparently permanently, and not take her things with her."

"Seemingly not."

"But her life is her own and she can do what she wants - yeh, I've got it." Griffiths pondered for a few minutes and continued, "What are the girl's names?"

Lees consulted his notebook. "The first is Adebanke and the second Muonasa."

"And their last names?"

"He doesn't know. Must have been tricky getting a credit rating on just a first name!" said the DS, laughing again.

"Actually, Lees, she wouldn't have been able to get one anyway because they have come from abroad."

"Oh," said Lees, feeling stopped in his tracks.

"Well, cast around; see if anyone knows girls by these names. Contact Immigration - they would have had to come in on a passport and their first names are unusual - well, maybe not from Nigeria, I don't know. But anyway see what turns up. But my guess is that, whatever you find, it won't be all that helpful because the girls got lost in the system, shall we call it, once they got here. Anyway, do your best."

"OK, will do."

A black lady in a simple grey, knee-length dress with unkempt hair and no make up walked into the police station.

"Can I help you?" said the officer in attendance.

" I would like to speak to Inspector Griffiths." "Please," she added. "Is he here?"

"I need to record some details. Could you give me your name?"

"Adebanke."

"And last name?"

She paused. "Smith."

"Smith?"

"Yes, Smith."

"OK. Let's leave it at that - Smith. And what is it about?"

"Please just tell him Adebanke is here. I think he will understand what it is all about."

Something about her manner, her demeanour, her searching gaze led the officer, against all his instincts, to bypass protocol.

"Is he here?" she asked.

"I will see if he is available," said the officer. "Please wait here." He pointed a finger towards her and walked into a back room. A few minutes later, he returned, porting a slightly smug smile.

"Well, it seems he is prepared to see you. Come this way." She shuffled behind him as he led her into DI Griffiths' office.

"Do sit down," said Griffiths, indicating a chair in front of his desk. Sitting behind it, and looking directly towards her, he began:

"Adebanke? Am I right?"

"Yes, sir."

"Forget the 'sirs', Adebanke. Tell me why you are here."

"I read the horrible news in one of the papers at the supermarket. It said you were looking for two girls, one called Adebanke and one called Muonasa."

"Yes, and?"

"Well, I am Adebanke."

"Were you living at the house with Muonasa?"

"Yes."

"But you left?" She did not answer. "Well, assuming from your silence that you did - and correct me if I am wrong - could you tell me why you did?"

"I'd rather not answer that. But I did know Muonasa."

"Where are you living now?" asked Griffiths.

"In a hostel."

Feeling bold, the DI thought he would probe: "A hostel for abused women?"

"Yes."

"Because of what you had been through?"

"Yes."

"Tell me about Muonasa."

"A lovely girl. Someone who should never have found herself in the place that she was. What has happened to her?"

"We don't know yet whether anything has happened to her. She left the house - as you did - so, for all we know, she might be as safe as you seem to be."

"But you think she might have been murdered?"

"Please tell me what you know about Muonasa," said Griffiths. "Did you know her well?"

"I saw her regularly since she arrived at the house a few months ago. We would talk, eat meals together, go out for walks or coffee. I am fairly sure I was her only real contact, apart from her brother who she met a few times - he's living in London - I think I could safely say I was her friend, her only friend. What has happened to her?"

"Where did you used to go, when you went out - for walks and coffee?"

"Just around the area. Often we'd have coffee at that Egyptian place down the road. I don't know if you know it."

"Yes. Where else? Was there anywhere she particularly liked to go or any people she particularly liked to meet?"

"She didn't really want to meet anyone. I was the only person she really spoke to - or confided in, at any rate. But she did like to go to the churchyard."

"Why?"

"She was quite a religious person, I think. Anglican. But she seemed fascinated by the gravestones. She liked to read what was written on them and fantasised about who they might have been and what lives they lived. In fact, apart from me, the people in those graves seemed to be the only ones that she related to."

"What about the brother?"

"I don't know much about him. He seems to be some bigwig in the oil business, currently stationed in London. Obviously, he's originally from Nigeria, like her, and the rest of the family is still there. She didn't talk a lot about him but she seemed to have mixed feelings about him. I might be guessing but I wonder if he is a bit of a control freak. She loved him as a brother but I think she might have been afraid of him too. Why are we talking about her as if she is definitely in the past?"

"Well, with respect, Adebanke, I am not."

"No, sorry. Somehow it just seems that she has gone. And someone has been murdered, so the papers say."

"Did she see anyone else regularly, apart from you and her brother?"

"She had medical consultations. She said that she had some sort of illness but I don't know what it was. She seemed healthy enough to me but she was adamant that she needed treatment so she was seeing someone regularly. She didn't talk about it very much but she seemed to rely on him quite a lot."

"Do you know his name or which hospital she went to?"

"No, I don't know his name. Or the hospital either but it must have been somewhere fairly close because I think she walked there."

"Anyone else that she had contact with?"

"She used to go and see the priest at the church. But, as I said, I think she was quite religious."

"Do you mean that she would see him on her own - outside of the normal church services?"

"Yes, I think so."

"Can you think of any reason why she would have chosen to leave the brothel of her own accord?"

"I know that, like me, she hated what she was doing there. But, where I managed to free my mind of it - well, most of the time, anyway - I think she felt it more deeply. I got the impression in the end that she was desperate to get out of it. I finally flipped when things started to go wrong - when I started working at the hotels. I suppose something could have flipped her too and prompted her to get out but, of course, I didn't see her towards the end so I cannot be sure."

"Well, Adebanke, I am very grateful that you have come in. You have helped enormously. Now, what about you? Which hostel are you in?"

"St. Matthew's on the Victoria Road."

"And you are being looked after?"

"Yes. They've given me these clothes, a bed and food. I am very grateful. But please don't tell anyone where I am."

"Why not?"

"Because someone would come and get me."

"Is that why you haven't gone back to the house for any of your belongings?"

"Yes."

"Do you feel that you are in danger?"

"Yes, maybe."

"OK, I'll make a note of that.   We won't reveal your address to anyone outside of the force but I may need to come back to you at some time for some further questions. Would it be OK if we came round to the hostel - surreptitiously, of course?"

"Yes, I'd like to help, if I can. I was very fond of her. I *am* very fond of her."

"Good. Can we escort you back?"

"No. I think it would be better if I went on my own."

"Oh, one more thing," he added, "Can you confirm your identity?"

"No, sorry, I can't.   But there are not many people who know about Muonasa, here in London. But I do. And I can't risk anything. Am I going to get into trouble?"

"No. You have helped us a lot. And we are after the big guys, not you."

"Well, good luck is all I can say."

Adebanke stood, waited for a few moments with head bowed, then sighed, shook her head, turned rapidly and walked out. Griffiths mirrored her movements - the sighing, the head shaking - then stared at his desk. "Bye!" he said, as she walked through the office door but she had gone. *Is this the time to study the social report?   Don't think I can face it. But something's got to be done about it. Later. Let's have some coffee.* He stood and walked into the kitchen.

Steve Griffiths felt some relief from the graveyard case because that day he had been called to a domestic dispute, apparently involving some violence. He parked his car, turned off the Beatles CD and paused for a moment. The DI's route from stress was to transport himself to the world of the 1960s.

A time when life was exciting, people felt freedom and each new day brought something new. Admittedly, he often thought to himself, he was not alive for most of it but he wished he had been. He bet police work would have been so much easier - just the odd person to pick up, dressed in strange clothes, high on drugs and acting in a bizarre fashion - no danger, a bit of cooling off; job done! Sadly, his sergeant did not share his tastes; he once told the DI that, amongst other things, he was into garage house music - whatever that is, thought the DI, and enquired no further. But now he was blessed with gang extortion, international trafficking, masterminded crime, drugs everywhere and most of it he had to ignore because it was insoluble. *And on my own patch too: brothels controlled from another country, girls being wrecked. And what do we do about it? Nothing.* As a kid, he'd loved the stories of Sherlock Holmes - the deduction, the insight, the cleverness. It was probably those tales that had drawn him to be a detective. He'd wished then he was Sherlock Holmes; still did.

But now he was at the house. DS Lees joined him as he walked up the path.

"Good morning. Glad you made it. Well, this might give us some relief, if that's what you can call it," said the DI.

"Why are we here?" asked Lees. "What happened to the uniforms?"

"They came last week to a previous event at this house and were turned away.   They thought we might be more approachable and, anyway, now it sounded like recurrent problems, we might want to look for evidence of a pattern of crime."

"Does that fit our job description?"

"It'll do."

As they knocked on the door, they both looked around the front of the house, the tiny front garden and the adjacent street.

"No car," said Lees.

"Quite so," said Griffiths. "We may find she is on her own. The eagle has flown the nest."

The door was opened by a woman in pyjamas, seemingly in her early 30s, with long, black shoulder-length hair, clearly unbrushed. But much more obvious to the two onlookers was her face: not only a picture of distress but also one, quite probably naturally pretty, but marred by bruises and open grazes to both cheeks and the left side of the chin. Tears that had streamed down her face had left red tracks as they had coursed over the open wounds. Scanning downwards, the DI noticed bruises, in red and purple, probably old, over the arms exposed beneath her short-sleeved pyjama top.   Looking further down, he noticed a few more bruises over the upper sides of both feet. *Where else on her body would we find them?* he thought.

After the normal formal introductions, the two men were allowed into the house and followed her into the small sitting room, scanning the area as they did so. Fairly normal, in so many respects: a settee, into which the woman had now slumped, a separate armchair, a television in the corner, but also, at the foot of a wall beneath a broken mirror, a fractured hi-fi system lying in pieces next to the skirting board. The paint and plaster on the wall between there and the mirror was fragmented, unlike the rest of the room, which was well decorated.

"We had a call from your neighbour who heard a lot of noise from your house and was worried about you. Did you know that?"

"Yes. She told me."

"And you don't object to our coming?"

"Not really, but I'm not sure what you can do, if anything."

"Well, why not tell us about it?"

"We had an argument and he walked out. We often have arguments; it's not unusual."

The two detectives enquired gently about the nature of their relationship, which was clearly vitriolic, but she offered little without prompting. After a few minutes, Griffiths decided to become more direct. "Mrs. Tennant...."

"Call me Tracey."

"Tracey, has he been violent to you? We have to know, not only because that is a criminal offence, but also because, if so, we have to consider ways to protect you, to prevent you from coming to further, possibly worse, harm."

"He's my husband; I am where I am. When you take on something, you have to live with it. Isn't that true about everything in life?"

"Well, no, Tracey, it isn't. Things can be changed. And there is no reason on earth why you should be a victim of violence. Has he been violent?"

Tracey started sobbing uncontrollably. Lees dragged a tissue from his pocket. "Sorry, it might not be that clean."

Disregarding the warning, she let her head drop forwards into the tissue held in both hands.

"He has a bad temper and I upset him easily."

"Has he been violent?" the DI persisted.

"I think sometimes he just can't control himself. I suggested he went to an anger management course but that just made him flare up. But I think it might be just the way he is."

"Has he hit you?"

"Yes, sometimes."

"Always in anger?"

Tracey let her hands drop and lifted her head. Her expression now open, she briefly flicked her hair and looked directly at the inspector. "Well, no actually. Our love-making has always been a bit rough - and that's been fine - but recently it's got more so, more than I would like, to be honest. I've asked him to calm down but he takes no notice. I sometimes wonder if he enjoys it more when I am upset."

"Is he responsible for these cuts and bruises I can see?"

Tracey looked down again, towards her lap. "Well, I didn't do them, I can tell you that."

"And he did?"

"Yes."

DI Griffiths leant forwards towards her and put his face close enough to hers to show concern without being intrusive.

"Tracey, this is serious. We often see this pattern of behaviour, with mounting violence, in a marital relationship, sadly almost always from the man to the woman. If it is allowed to carry on, it will probably get worse. I hate to say this, and I don't want to alarm you, but he may end up killing you."

Tracey looked up again. "Oh, I don't think he'd ever intend to do that!"

"As you said, he may not be able to stop himself, especially if he is getting some sort of gratification from it." She said nothing but continued looking downwards.

"Do you want to make a formal complaint? Because our hands are pretty much tied if you don't."

"No, no, I can't," she said, shaking her head.

"Why not?"

"I just can't."

"Because you are frightened of him?"

"I can't. I really can't," she said with mounting distress in her voice.

"Are you prepared to make a statement, confirming what you have told me so far?"

"No."

The inspector sighed heavily and looked away from her, towards his sergeant. The DI said nothing but it was obvious to Lees that his boss was intensely frustrated and probably unsure what to do next. Lees had worked with him long enough to know that he hated being thwarted. Although Griffiths was good at taking the practical route when necessary, he had a rather idealistic view of how the police service and the judicial system should work, a view sadly not reflected in average human behaviour.

For the next few minutes, the inspector persisted in his attempts to persuade her, promising confidentiality, dealing with a female police officer, protection from the press and any other qualifier that his experience in the force had taught him. But to no avail. Eventually, the two detectives were obliged to make their exit, leaving Tracey Tennant sitting on the settee, the DI's tissue in hand, staring at the floor.

"Supposing we come back to see how you are tomorrow?" he added, as he was leaving.

"Please don't," she said quietly.

Outside the house, the two men stood for a few minutes before getting into their respective cars.

"That's not right," said Lees, knowing that Griffiths would agree with him.

"It certainly isn't," said Griffiths. "We've got to do something about this. The domestic violence business is turning into an epidemic and I wonder if we, as a force - or even as a national police service - are just ignoring it."

"But, although it's a crime in its own right," said Lees, "if she won't press charges, we've got no evidence. We can be pretty confident he's not going to confess to anything. And it's not just a domestic business, is it?"

"No, it isn't," said Griffiths reflectively. "I'll tell you, Lees, that social report that's sitting on my desk and which, I am sorry to say, I keep passing over, highlights the same problem amongst prostitutes - they are often victims of violence from clients with what can only be described as perversions. And what about the whole prostitute business in itself, Lees? We just turn a blind eye to it. Why? Because it's difficult to sort out and we don't want the press latching onto gory stories of immorality and twisted minds, endemic here in Britain, and the police powerless to do anything about it! So we ignore it. Well, today has taught me one thing, Lees: I'm going to go back to the station and think about what we can do about this poor lady we have just seen. And I'm going to study that social report. And together, one way or another, we are going to bring these nasties to justice. Isn't it weird that it's easier to deal with a case of violence against a woman when she has been murdered because then we have a major crime, the victim cannot object to police involvement and the evidence is there in the form of the dead body?"

"Is it?" said Lees, thinking back to the body in the graveyard.

Steve Griffiths got back into his car, sat for a while, then fastened his seatbelt and turned on the Beatles CD. As "I Feel Fine" poured through the speakers, he turned up the volume and thought, *Maybe it really was easier back then,* before driving back to the station.

Lees visited all of the three hospitals within walking distance of the brothel and, as usual, met obstruction at every turn. At the first two hospitals, his pleas to the receptionist to direct him to any consultant who had treated Nigerian women within the previous three months met a bureaucratic barrier. She was not in a position to answer his queries, she explained. He would probably need to speak to the chief executive or one of his designated authorities. She also pointed out that, although she was in no position to comment, she wondered if some kind of warrant may be necessary because patients' medical records were strictly confidential; that much she knew. Lees did indeed know the appropriate protocols but he had learned that bypassing those procedures, wherever possible, and without confrontation, could often speed things along. But things were tightening up; old-fashioned police methods of winging it were increasingly being blocked.

Fortunately, at the third hospital, St. Joseph's Hospital, he had a break. At the moment that he uttered "consultants treating Nigerian women in the last three months", Dr. Haynes walked by and overheard. Something prompted him to stop. The receptionist was about to utter what Lees feared would be the standard response when Dr. Haynes stopped walking and waved his hand to quieten the girl.

"Can I help you?" he said and, after a pause, "Sorry, I am one of the consultants here."

Lees produced his identity card and explained that he was investigating a possible murder. One lead was Nigerian women who may have been treated at one of the nearby hospitals recently.

"Come into my office," said Mark Haynes.

Pretty obviously a private hospital, thought the detective, as he walked through the door and scanned the room bigger than his own sitting room at home, the antique oak desk (*might be fake*) and the fine cotton, patterned curtains. He accepted the doctor's invitation to take a seat (*another nice chair - looks to be oak - but this might be fake too, I suppose*). He declined the offer of coffee.

After further introductions from both sides, Lees explained that the detective force was investigating a possible murder case. As yet, the precise identity of the person deceased was unknown but forensic evidence suggested that the body (*body? Is that overstating the case for a bundle of ash?*) was female and African. They had other evidence concerning a missing person who would fit that description and who had recently received medical attention from one of the hospitals in the area. They were now attempting to trace any such individuals.

"Are you able to assist?" asked the sergeant.

"Well, it's a bit of a long shot, Sergeant, if I may say so. I have had a number of consultations with Nigerian women over recent months. There are also many other Nigerian women in this area and statistically one or more of them will have had hospital consultations too. However, yes, there is one currently attending my clinic but I would not want you to jump to the conclusion that she is the person you seek. "

"Don't worry about that, sir; we are used to examining the evidence carefully before coming to a conclusion."

"Yes, of course."

"How often do you see her?"

"About once per week."

"And the last time?"

"I think about twelve days ago or so. I can check if it's important."

"Well, it may be ultimately. But twelve days ago - from what you say, am I right in thinking that that is longer than would usually occur between visits?"

How much should I tell him? thought Haynes. *The last thing I want is for all this to backfire. How much of our relationship and its effect on my family is going to come out? And what about the letter? What will they make of that? Above all, I have to protect my daughter, my wife, my family. Maybe just go easy.*

"Yes, she missed an appointment last week," he said hurriedly.

"You sure about that?"

"Certain."

"Do you mind if I take a look at your appointments diary? It's just that the precise dates may turn out to be important."

"I am afraid I don't have it with me. But I can bring it to you if necessary."

"Is it not computerised?" said Lees, glancing across to the doctor's desktop machine.

"Yes, but I do not keep the database on my computer. It is in the central office, where appointments are made."

"May I have her name and address?"

"As you know, Sergeant, we in medicine have a responsibility to maintain confidentiality. Indeed, if I am not mistaken, it is now a legal requirement."

"I do, sir, but you probably also know that we can gain legal authority for release of the medical records if there is a justifiable reason."

"Yes. And, of course, if such authority were to be issued, I would willingly comply. But, on what seems so far to be a casual enquiry, if I may say so, I feel obliged to respect my patient's interests."

"I understand. Well, thank you, Doctor Haynes, I won't take up any more of your time. But I trust you will be content for me to return, if necessary, to ask you further questions. And we may well need to see those medical records but, as you point out, we will gain the necessary authority first." He smiled unconvincingly, stood up and extended his hand. Mark Haynes failed in his normal reflex to return a handshake because his mind was distracted. *They will question Rebecca and Amy, I know. Somehow I've got to stop them finding out about them. But how? And that letter! Why did I not just walk past the detective when he stood at reception? What made me respond? And Muonasa - silly girl!*

"Goodbye for the moment," from the sergeant brought Mark back to consciousness.

"Sorry, yes indeed! Goodbye - for the moment!" And he grasped the sergeant's hand and shook it vigorously.

As soon as he was sure that the detective had left the room, Mark collapsed into his chair and put his head in his hands. *Why did I ever take her on?*

Lees returned to his car. Of course, he knew, from Adebanke's evidence, that the girl's name was Muonasa but something in his mind had led him to withhold that knowledge to see what the doctor might offer unprompted. And it was clearly not very much. But then again, it was Dr. Haynes who had volunteered to speak to him. *Maybe I am being too suspicious,* he thought. *But then again there is something about him.....*The DS set off to report to his inspector with a determination that they would get the authority to look at the medical records.

"Thank you, Lees. Very helpful," said DI Griffiths. "Since your report, without too much probing, I have managed to find out a bit about Dr. Haynes. He is a consultant psychiatrist, with sessions, as you know, at the private hospital St. Joseph's. He is married with a teenager daughter and regularly attends St. Francis' church. That led me to think: Adebanke, her friend who came in to see us, said she was very religious. She would not have known about the churches in the area when she first arrived here. Is it just possible that she got a recommendation from her treating doctor - Haynes - and attended the same church as him? Maybe worth some enquiries. And definitely, yes, we need to get hold of those medical records. If it is Dr. Haynes who has been treating her, and he is a psychiatrist, could she have had some mental disorder that led her to suicide?"

"Great!" said Lees. "It sounds as if we have a good enough case to get that authority."

"I think so."

"I'll get on with it."

Griffiths picked up the social report that had been lying on his desk, half read, for too long, he thought. He went over the passages that he had read previously but this time with a lot more care. There was an increasingly flourishing trade, he read, of prostitution at the hotels in the area, usually involving business men on temporary stays. The suspicion was that the word was spreading around the darker side of the grapevine that the area was a good place to stay because of the services that were available here. The main business area was a few miles away but the attraction of this area meant that the hotels nearer the workplaces were being used less whilst the ones in this locale were showing a significant rise in occupancy. The distance from work was not a problem because of the good public transport services and, no doubt, because business expenses would cover taxi fares.

Evidence suggested that the supply of prostitutes stemmed from a few houses in one or two streets. Most of the women there were Nigerian. The houses were within comfortable walking distance of the hotels but the traffic seemed to involve exclusively women travelling from brothel to hotel, rather than men going from hotel to brothel. This was perhaps not surprising, said the report, because the men would be keen to preserve their anonymity. *You don't say*, thought Griffiths.

The hotel managers and, in some cases, owners appeared to be content with this arrangement because of the increase in business, which offset any concern they may have concerning a decline in the perceived standard of their accommodation. *Money talks.*

More recently, however, the situation appeared to have changed - or, at least, entered a new phase. The authors of the report were aware of evidence of increasing violence imparted to the women from the clients. The concern was that this represented a new trend in the pattern of behaviour between the women and their clients and, more so, that the hotels in this locale were now becoming a centre for this particularly unpleasant form of sexual activity. The increasing trend, which was continuing, suggested that word was spreading across the dark grapevine - *"dark grapevine" - that's the second time they've used that phrase - not sure I've ever heard it before but it's quite good; I must remember it* - and thereby attracting more men inclined to that behaviour.

One of the most troublesome features of the situation is that the violent behaviour may not be consensual. The authors of the report had no direct evidence that it was not but the nature of some of the injuries reported were quite severe and arguably beyond the realm of passive acceptance.

The hotel proprietors were becoming aware of increasing noise levels emanating from the bedrooms, which concerned them. A generous interpretation would be that this concern centred around the welfare of the women but a cynic may argue that their primary objectives were preservation of their businesses and avoidance of clashes with the authorities.

The report concluded that action needed to be taken to interrupt this trend. Already there seemed to be a number of cases that would amount to grievous bodily harm but, if the pattern were left unchecked, the police might well find themselves presented with a murder case. *Maybe we already have*, thought the inspector.

Inspector Griffiths smiled, put down the file and took another slurp of coffee. *Not much doubt about that one*, he said to himself. *I think the CPS should be happy - and unless they get another twisted barrister to defend him, he should go down for some time.* He made one final scan of his checklist and flow diagram. *Seen running from the scene of the crime by two credible witnesses; the body in the shop had his DNA on it; the watches found in his flat were of a make sold in only three jewellers in the area; and he had no explanation of why he would want five watches and how he could afford to pay for them. No doubt, his team will go for manslaughter but a charge of murder should stick.*

"You're looking happy," said Lees, as he walked into the office.

"Think we've got the Stanton Jewellers case sewn up!" said the DI, smiling even more broadly.

"Great!" said the sergeant. "Well, here are a couple more things for you to think about. Don't want you being idle!"

"Thanks."

"First off, I have got the medical records and had a look through them. No doubt you will want to examine them in detail but, to me, it doesn't make a lot of sense and, in fact, it all sounds a bit weird. It seems that she has some sort of mental disorder - no surprise there; remember Haynes is a psychiatrist. She was advised to come to London by someone, a doctor I assume, in Nigeria. I'm no medical expert but the symptoms he told her she would likely develop without treatment sound horrific, certainly nothing like I've come across in any of our cases that went through forensic psychiatry. I'd be interested to know what you make of it. Anyway, perhaps more important from our point of view is that I can see no mention that Haynes thought she was a suicide risk."

"Thanks, Lees. As you say, that may be the most important observation. I will certainly take a look and, if necessary, get our medical experts to add their opinion on it - and the rest of the business you describe. What's the second thing?"

"The burned body in the graveyard - remember the stone? Well, we've got a letter from the hack at the Telegraph who thinks he's got some ideas about it. Remember the guy? Julian Harcourt-Brown, he's called. He picked up some stuff from us early on in the case."

"I was feeling happy," said the DI, "until you came in. All I need right now is some chap from the press waxing on about a stone. Haven't we got more important things to worry about? And the name, Julian Harcourt-Brown? Is that Eton? Or alternatively could it be Eton?"

The DS laughed. "Well, actually what he is interesting, if nothing else."

"If nothing else - quite! Let me see it."

Dear Inspector Griffiths,

I trust you will not take exception to my writing to you unprompted but, as you may recall, I have taken great interest in the case of the burnt body in the graveyard, on which you have been working. I was made aware that a stone had initially been observed at the scene of the (presumed) crime but that later inspections showed it to have disappeared. I was fortunate to have learned that the stone was decorated so, when I discovered that the body was believed to have been of West-African extraction, I enquired of my sister who is an expert in African anthropology.

Her observations are as follows: essentially, based upon her knowledge of the subject, she conceives of two possible significances to the stone. The first is that it is a religious object, indeed a sacred object because some devotees of the Yoruba religion, which is, shall we say, endemic in that area, actually believe that God somehow resides in, or influences, particular objects. She may therefore have believed that, by carrying the stone with her, she literally had God by her side.

The second is more trivial but nonetheless may provide a means of identifying more accurately the identity of the victim. The notion is that the stone is a good luck charm, based upon a longstanding folk tale about a magic stone that protected the carrier from evil.

Either way, it might appear that the victim was carrying the stone to keep her from harm, either through genuine holy involvement or the more superstitious influence of 'luck'. However, perhaps an additionally important observation of my sister is that both of these beliefs, the divine and the superstitious, are most firmly grounded in Nigeria. Thus, if my sister is correct, and she would be the first to admit that her observations may be seen as conjectural, the identity of the victim would most likely be Nigerian.

Again I would say that the purpose of my writing to you was entirely in an attempt to be helpful and I trust that you do not take exception. Naturally, if you wish to discuss any of these matters further, do not hesitate to contact me.

With best wishes

Yours sincerely,

Julian Harcourt-Brown

"Yes, Eton, I would say," said the inspector, as he put down the letter.

"Oh, come on, boss," said Lees, laughing again. "So, Cheltenham College is just a run-of-the-mill comprehensive, is it? That's where you went, wasn't it?"

"Thank you, Lees. Actually, what he says is quite interesting, as you suggest, though I'm not sure it takes us much further."

"It adds to the idea that she was Nigerian."

"True. Don't think a court of law would buy it but, yes, it does help our thinking. Not that I would ever admit that to the press!"

"Perish the thought!" Lees laughed even more loudly. He liked his boss but had to admit that sometimes he could be a bit quirky.

Dear Julian,

I am sorry not to have replied to your last letter before now but I have been distracted by a lot of goings-on here in the Faculty. Our professor suddenly declared that he was moving to a new post in Nairobi with, can you believe it, three months' notice! Hardly time to recruit a replacement without the Department being left void of a head for a while. Not only that but one of our senior lecturers had organised a year's sabbatical some time ago and started it almost exactly at the time that our professor left. That has left me to hold the fort - or, at least, quite a lot of it.

Anyway, the students have now gone on vacation so I have found myself with a bit more time, at least until I have to get the appraisals of their last year's work ready for the next term. So I thought quite a bit about you (always good) and your most recent endeavour.

The stone! Well, I have given you my ideas previously but what I had not realised until I researched it (Yoruba is not my area of expertise) was that one of the gods praised by some in the Yoruba religion is Shango. He is the god of thunder and lightning. One of the things that he does, particularly when he creates the thunder, is to send stones down to earth, which the priests collect and deify. They believe that these stones have supernatural powers even to the extent that they enshrine them in the temples of the gods.

I know I have told you previously that some Nigerians consider some stones to have supernatural powers but I did not know the bit about the stones falling to earth from the sky. Let's say that the girl found the stone somewhere, maybe after a thunderstorm, and simply kept it to give her good fortune.

That might have created considerable anger amongst some of the Yoruba people if the priests wanted to enshrine it in a temple, assuming they knew she had it. I don't imagine such horrific vengeance would be intended by the priests or most of the people because my understanding is that Yoruba is basically peaceful and tolerant. However, sadly we know that some people of all religions act extremely, supposedly in the name of their faith.

I tell you this because it might put a new complexion on the whole matter of why that girl would hold a seemingly ordinary stone so close to her. And there might be some people who believe that it had a controlling power over her and others who wanted to seek revenge on her for having kept it.

It's all a bit tangential, I know, and I doubt that these thoughts are likely to help the police much in their search for the perpetrator of the death but I know how much the case has fascinated you - and, to some extent your enthusiasm has spread across continents, well to me at least! So I hope that this information at least stimulates your mind and thereby keeps you out of mischief!

Much love,

Sarah

Chapter 11

Detective Sergeant Lees was quite proud of himself. When he had gone to Dr. Haynes' hospital to pick up the copies of the medical records authorised by the court, he decided to pop into the office of Dr. Haynes' secretary. He had gone, he explained, simply to express his thanks on behalf of Inspector Griffiths and himself for the time spent the other day in informal interview. Naturally, he took the time to engage in some casual conversation while he was there, including how much the secretary enjoyed working at the hospital, how busy she was and so on and he was glad to learn that she was very pleased to have a job there, especially working with Dr. Haynes, who was a charming man. As the conversation unfolded, she explained that he was a man of principle, possibly based upon his strong Christian beliefs. It did not take much further effort from the sergeant to discover the name and location of his regular church. *Bullseye!* thought Lees. In order not to arouse too much suspicion, he declined to ask whether the female Nigerian patient attended the same church but, given the willingness of his secretary to share information, he had no difficulty in envisaging the scenario in which she had told the same facts to Muonasa.

Lees was no church-going man but he did appreciate architecture. *Nobody makes buildings like this anymore*, he thought, as he approached the neo-Gothic front of St. Francis and stopped for a few minutes to look at the two gargoyles that faced down from the line of the roof. *Not bad for a small district - and who, if anyone, were those guys up there?* He pondered for a while as to what kind of community would have warranted such a church, not grand in the overall scheme of things but impressive for where it was. He opened the heavy, creaking, oak door and entered the body of the church, scanned the rows of traditional wooden pews and shifted his gaze towards the altar. Two rows of choir stalls lined the vestibule between the pews and the altar - *What's the name for that space? Is that the nave?* Behind the altar was a large stained-glass window in a vertically orientated rectangular shape with a semicircular top. The red, blue and yellow panes depicted Christ on the cross, which he assumed was not unusual, but more interesting were the surrounding panes showing a variety of animals, one of which, a dog, was obviously dead. Others showed sheep and cows. *Originally, a farming community, I guess.*

Until now, he had taken the whole atmosphere as one and was not overtly conscious of the music but then he noticed the organist, fingers gesticulating, body swaying and feet seemingly marching on the pedals beneath. He smiled and took a deep breath. *Impressive, very impressive - enough to make you a Christian!*

"It's a wonderful window, isn't it?" said a voice from behind.

Startled, Lees turned round abruptly. "Oh, hello - yes, very. Altogether, a lovely church!"

"Yes, we are very fortunate. I assume you are a visitor - I don't recall seeing you before and I'm quite good with faces. Sorry, I'm the churchwarden here. Patricia Peters - pleased to meet you."

"Thank you. David Lees. Pleased to meet you too."

"Is there anything I can tell you about our church?"

"Well, to be honest, I'm here - apart from admiring your beautiful church - as part of an investigation." He produced his identity card, which the churchwarden examined with care, and asked if she would be willing to answer a few questions.

"Nothing much dramatic happens here," she said with a slight snigger. "No doubt some members of the congregation wished it did but we still run a fairly traditional ministry."

"It's just the congregation that I'd like to ask you about. Nothing too threatening."

"Very well. I'll try to help but I cannot betray confidences."

"No, indeed. All I'd like to know is whether Dr. Haynes is a regular member of your church."

"Well, I don't suppose there's any harm. Yes, he is one of our most regulars - a devoted, truly Christian man who would do anything for anyone. He has run some of our pastoral groups although less so recently. He's very good at it and we wish he would do more but I imagine he's just too busy."

"And do you know a lady called Muonasa? She's Nigerian."

"Yes, I do! She's been coming just relatively recently but seems keen."

"Every Sunday?"

"Yes, although, since you mention it, I don't remember seeing her for the last week or two."

"Did she fit in well?"

"We welcome anyone who is interested in worshipping God or who, in fact, feels the call to church for whatever reason."

"Yes, I'm sure that is the church's policy. But did everyone in the congregation share those views about her?"

"Yes, I think so," she said hesitatingly.

"You think so?"

"Well, mostly definitely. But she is, you know, a little bit different from others in the congregation and, for some people, it takes a little time to adjust to someone new, even though their intentions are good."

"Because she was black?"

"She was the only black member in our church - and, of course, not only that but she was a visitor from another country. But I cannot believe that would pose a problem for most people. They might take more time to get to know her because, well, her culture and habits may be a little different from ours in this sleepy hamlet." She smiled in attempted reassurance but Lees persisted.

"Not really a hamlet, is it? And probably not that sleepy. But anyway, if I may, can I ask you not to think about 'most people' but anyone who seemed to have more than an average grudge against her - or who seemed to take exception to her for whatever reason."

"No, I cannot think of anyone. Well, Amy didn't seem to take to her very much but then she's just a teenager and, as you probably know, they get all sorts of funny ideas as they are growing up."

"Amy?"

"Dr. Haynes' daughter. It's nothing really and I can't put my finger on what seemed wrong. It just seemed that she resented Muonasa's presence. But, as I said, that might well be what you would expect from someone of her age. I'm sure there is nothing in it."

"Maybe not," said Lees, reflectively.

There was something about the churchwarden's expression and demeanour that led the sergeant to suspect that she was not being as forthcoming in response to the last question as she might but he knew that he was unlikely to make much more progress on this first meeting. He thanked Mrs. Peters, congratulated her again on the quality of the church and said goodbye. *She knows I'll be back,* he thought, *and, by then, she will have prepared something better to say - something factual but delivered in a way that does not implicate anyone as a possible creator of mischief.*

After Detective Sergeant Lees had left, Patricia Peters sat in one of the pews, closed her eyes and prayed. After a few minutes, she looked up towards the stained glass window at the front and studied each pane in turn, finally focussing on the image of Christ. *We have to do good, that's all we have to do - and show love.*

She stood and walked briskly into the church office by the side of the main building. She sat at the desk and picked up the telephone receiver.

"Patricia Peters. He will know who I am. Yes, please, if it's convenient, please put me through."

"Hello, Patricia," said Dr. Haynes. "Nice to hear your voice. What can I do for you? I know I keep promising to start the pastoral class again for new church members but I have recently just been rushed off my feet."

"Yes, I know Mark. And, no, it's not that. I just felt I had to speak to you. It may all be nothing but a detective came into church this afternoon, making enquiries as part of an investigation, as he called it. He didn't say what. But he asked about that girl Muonasa and who, in particular, seemed to dislike her or bear a grudge about her. He mentioned your name too. Obviously, I told him what a devoted man you were and I don't think he had anything against you. But when he asked about who may bear a grudge, I couldn't help thinking about Amy. I hope you do not mind my saying so, because I think you know, but Amy has on occasions seemed a bit hostile towards her. I remember a few times that Rebecca had to drag her away for fear that Amy might say something she shouldn't. I don't know why and it's none of my business but the last thing you and your family need is some detective snooping around you, your wife and your daughter on a wild goose chase. It would be very upsetting and I don't imagine it would help Amy's mental state very much. I know you have talked about her worries in confidence to me. Sorry if this is all nothing but I thought I had better mention it. At least to prepare you if nothing else."

"Did you tell the detective any of this? About Amy and so on?"

"No, of course not," said Patricia, with perhaps just a little too much emphasis. "And he does not know that I have phoned you. I told him that I did not know anyone who would bear a grudge against Muonasa. And that's basically true. I don't know enough about anyone to say confidently that they bear a grudge. And naturally I include Amy in that. I was just worried that things could escalate out of control to the good of no-one."

"Thank you, Patricia. See you soon."

Mark put down the phone, sat down, looked towards the window with elbows on the desk and chin in his hands and thought. *What went wrong? She was a charming, lovely child with the whole world before her. We used to play games together and everything seemed normal. I was busy, yes, but that's what medicine does for you and I was always there for her - at least, I hope so. But now, it's all changed. What on earth has gone wrong?*

He breathed heavily, looked up to the ceiling and then back to the window. *Come on, Mark, you're a psychiatrist - you know. It may be the drugs; it may be a mental illness; it may be both; and it could be just her - creation of a mixed pattern of genes. Whatever, that's what you've got. But why has she taken it out on, to her, an unknown girl from Nigeria? Deluded, I guess, and unfortunately dangerously so. But you've already taken steps to protect Amy - and the family - and you cannot stop now.*

He picked up the phone and called Rebecca.

"Where's Amy?"

"At Lucy's. Why?"

"I thought we'd tried to put a stop to that. We know what goes on when she goes round there. And she's supposed to be on a rehabilitation programme. Going round to Lucy's, with just the two of them on their own, doesn't help that very much, I'd say."

"Mark, I can't put a ball and chain on her ankle. I am doing everything I can to help her - have done and always would. Is that the reason you called?"

"No. The police have been round to the church, enquiring about Muonasa." He did not get much further before Rebecca interjected: "Don't talk to me about that woman. She just caused misery to our family and particularly our daughter - and, frankly, I don't think you helped much by your actions. As usual, it's down to me to look after my daughter and do whatever is necessary to give her peace of mind."

"Well, the girl Muonasa has not been around for a while, has she?" said Mark. "But the important point is that they are looking for anyone who might have had a grudge against her - and Amy will appear first in the firing line."

"A justifiable grudge perhaps," said Rebecca.

"Well, not justifiable in fact, but, justifiable or not, it would not remove the implication of guilt."

"We just tell the police that we read about the death of someone in the graveyard, who later investigation identified as a probable Nigerian woman," said Rebecca. "We hadn't seen Muonasa for a while and put two and two together that the dead body was her. All that is true - or potentially so. The fact that Amy may not have liked her very much is neither here nor there, particularly since we - or Lucy - can account for all of her actions over the last few weeks. She has been on holiday from school for most of it so that's easy."

"OK. Just be aware that the police may come knocking and the last thing Amy needs is a murder accusation against her."

"Come home when you can spare the time," she said with loaded sarcasm. "As you know, I'm never sure what you get up to all these hours away."

"Working, Becky, working. For that matter, I'm not sure what you get up to when I am not there. See you later."

"Goodbye."

Griffiths and Lees were back at the brothel, with some trepidation. They sensed from previous interviews, albeit brief, that Adedayo had a fragment of decency, which was a weakness in his profession. But they also knew that he was skilled in clouding the truth in obfuscation and sidetracks, almost certainly directed by an overpowering fear for his own safety. Lees asked his superior why the force could not direct their attention to the guys who were controlling the whole operation and break up the sordid business from the top downwards but Griffiths explained patiently that it would be necessary to involve the Nigerian authorities because it was in that country where the power base lay. Apart from the political difficulties, which were beyond the control of the police, he suspected that nobody really wanted to know, either in Nigeria or in this country, for that matter.

"Maybe we can get him in a weak moment," said the inspector, as they approached the front door.

Adedayo answered their repeated knocks by opening the door a few inches and gazing around it; once again, he was not expecting any more clients that day and few other people ever came to call.

"Ah, hello again!" he said with an exaggerated smile.

"May we come in?"

Adedayo gave a quick glance around the hall and up the stairs, listened for a few moments but, hearing nothing, opened the door wider. The detectives entered the narrow hall. Looking around, they noticed a staircase up to the left and a half open door to the room directly ahead. Just within view in that room was a desk, on which lay a leather-backed book. While Griffiths engaged in preliminary chat with Adedayo, Lees ambled down the hall towards the open door and picked up the book, a diary. He had just managed to flick through a few pages, scattered with names, all men, each listed against the name of another, in each case a woman, before Adedayo intervened.

"Sorry, that's private," he said, snatching the diary and placing it tightly under his left armpit.

"OK," said Lees. "Maybe we will get to examine it later." Then, staring threateningly into Adedayo's eyes, added: "Unless it mysteriously disappears - but I don't imagine that will happen, do you?" Adedayo gave no reply but turned back to the inspector.

"How can I help you?"

"We have talked before about a girl who used to live here but apparently left for no reason. Her name was Muonasa."

"Yes, yes, I remember it well. And?"

"And we are led to believe that she has a brother living in London. Do you know anything about that?"

Adedayo pondered for a while. *Is there anything to lose by telling them about him? The brother might tell them about her goings on here but it's pretty obvious they know about them already and, so far, they haven't closed us down. As long as the money keeps going into the coffers of the powers that be, they probably never will either. Can't think of any other reason - and it may be that this brother's rantings will keep them occupied for a while and away from us.*

"Yes. She went out to meet him, for dinner I think."

"Do you know who he is?"

"Not exactly. But I think she said his name was Obaloluwa Apparently, he works for some big oil company."

"Anything else?"

Griffith's question was drowned by the sound of a cry from one of the upstairs bedrooms.

"One of the residents is unwell," said Adedayo. "Colic, I think. What did you say?"

"I said do you know anything else about this brother?" said Griffiths, ignoring the interruption.

"No, sorry. That's all I know. Oh, I believe he is a devout Christian."

"Which church? Was it the one Muonasa attended?"

"Don't know. Sorry. But I don't think she ever met him at church so I suppose not."

"Thank you," said the inspector. "I don't think there is any point in taking up any more of your time."

Outside the house, Lees stopped the DI on the way back to the car. "Why didn't you grill him some more? He's obviously hiding a mine of information. What about that diary? That might have told us something. And that cry from upstairs - shouldn't we have gone to investigate?"

"Lees," replied Griffiths, "that man lives a life of subterfuge. The diary would simply list a load of sad men with dates when they can come round to get sex where they are incapable of getting it anywhere else - and prepared to pay for it. Have you ever felt the need to pay for sex? Come to think of it, don't answer that! No, he would never write down anything that might backfire on him. He doesn't care about running a diary of prostitution because he knows we are not going to do anything about it - sadly. And, as for the cry, he told us a reason - crap, I agree - but without a just cause and preferably a warrant, our hands are a bit tied - for the moment, at least. And we don't want to put him off helping us in our main enquiry by probing, if you will forgive the phrase, exactly what is going on upstairs when we can pretty much guess what it is anyway. Softly, softly..."

"Catchee monkey," said Lees.

"Exactly!"

"Sorry, that sounds a bit racist," said the DS.

"Oh, come on, Lees, cut the political correctness - it's a saying," said Griffiths. "Now, let's get serious. There cannot be many Nigerian men with a first name of Obaloluwa, working in one of the major oil industries with a base in London. Search them out - and find the brother."

"Will do," said Lees. "What do you think he knows?"

"No idea. Until we ask. Oh, and some time, we've got to go round to see Dr. Haynes, his wife and his daughter. I'll fix it up. You get on with the brother."

Griffiths got back into his car, started the engine and picked up a random CD to put into the player. As he drove off and the music started, Los Bravos sang "*Black is black; I want my baby back...*" *How ironic,* thought the DI.

At one point during the interview, the detective inspector wondered who was asking and who was answering the questions, because Dr. Haynes had taken on a much more aggressive role than the DI had expected from their earlier encounter. Defensive would be an understatement. Griffiths' experience naturally led him to question why. After all, following a few questions exploring a little further how Muonasa had come to be under the consultant's care and what was his longer term plan, he had only asked for an interview with the whole family, including Haynes' wife and daughter, at their home. He had not even yet examined the medical records that Lees had given him, deciding to do that in preparation for the meeting with the whole family, in case something about Muonasa's medical condition could have led to the antipathy from Haynes' daughter reported to Lees by the churchwarden. But it was the mention of the family that seemed to ignite the doctor's passion. *Maybe just natural concern,* thought Griffiths - *or maybe not.*

"Why do you want to meet my family?" asked Haynes. "And especially my daughter. What's she got to do with anything?"

"Do you have any reason to suspect that she might have something against Muonasa?"

"What?! She's a young girl, Inspector. People of that age have grudges against anything that does not fit with their idea of life. Teenagers live in a world of their own. Do you have any children, may I ask?"

"So, is that yes or no?"

"Inspector, you are not, I hope, suggesting that a teenage girl - my daughter - could have anything to do with the disappearance and death of a Nigerian prostitute who happened to be my patient!"

"I don't recall mentioning anything about prostitution or death," said the DI.

"You don't need to. It's obvious. And, anyway, your sergeant told me, about the death at least. OK, yes, I knew Muonasa was a prostitute and I am sorry for having said it in the heat of the moment because that should be part of her confidential medical record as far as I am concerned. And, as for her death, like everyone else who reads the newspapers, I am aware of a burnt body found in the graveyard which leads you to come and ask me about a patient of mine who has gone missing. And, as I said, your sergeant has already done so. Not difficult to put two and two together, is it?"

"So, to go back to my earlier question, do you have any reason to suspect that your daughter might have something against Muonasa?"

"No. No, I do not."

"Then you will not object to my coming round to talk to her and your wife? You know that I can enforce an interview if necessary but it would be much better for everyone, especially your daughter, if it were all done voluntarily - and calmly."

Dr. Haynes fell silent. After a few minutes, he said, "Very well. But let me warn them first."

"Of course. I will contact you tomorrow. May I have your mobile number?"

Mark burst into the house and slammed the front door behind him.

"What's wrong with you?" said Rebecca, rushing from the sitting room.

"Where's Amy?" said Mark.

"At Lucy's."

"Oh God, not again! Look, I've had Inspector Griffiths nosing round and he wants to come and interview you and Amy. So far, he hasn't raised any concerns about you but, as we suspected, he is homing in on Amy. He wants to know if she had anything against Muonasa."

"Well, she never leaves home so we can reassure him that she couldn't have been involved in anything to do with her disappearance."

"Becky! She is at Lucy's as we speak! She was at Lucy's when I warned you in the telephone call. From now on, until this police investigation has gone away, she cannot leave the house!"

"We can try, Mark, but you know she has problems that we are trying to deal with. And she might be difficult to control until we have sorted out those problems. To put it simply, she might just walk out."

"True," he said, becoming calmer. "In fact, if they find out that the only place she ever goes is to Lucy's and that is to take drugs, that in itself may make them ease off. Of course, if the news got out, it might not help us - or particularly my role at the hospital - but she might be let off the hook."

"Mark, can you stop thinking of your career for just one moment?"

"If you remember, it does pay the mortgage."

"There is one other thing," said Becky. "She has to get the drugs from somewhere so sometimes she would have been wandering the streets. As we know, the places she will have visited are not that far away from where Muonasa lived. I guess the police will soon latch onto that."

"Oh,God!"

"Please stop blaspheming, Mark," said Becky. "It doesn't help."

"Well, Becky, at least we two know for sure that Amy had nothing to do with Muonasa's death. Whatever it takes, we just have to convince the police of that. She has enough to worry about."

"Exactly!"

Chapter 12

"Have we heard any more about that stone?" asked Griffiths. "Has anyone found it yet?"

"I didn't think you were all that excited about it. And, no, it still seems to be AWOL."

"I'm not very excited about it, Lees, but there is something odd about it. Why was she carrying it? If as that journalist says, it was to protect her from harm, harm from what or whom?"

"Oh, lots of people carry things like that, don't they, with nothing specific in mind. There used to be a big fashion for people to wear St. Christopher medals to look after them when they were travelling. It may be no more than that."

"That's true. But why would it disappear? Surely someone has moved it; it could hardly do so on its own unless there really is more to this than even I can imagine."

"I like the 'even I' bit, boss!"

Ignoring his subordinate, the inspector continued: "And, if someone did move it, it might just have their fingerprints or DNA on it - and that may be quite helpful. Agreed?"

"Agreed, most definitely."

"Just ask forensics, scene of crime and uniforms that they haven't got it somewhere - even in someone's locker or pocket. Don't be too hard on them - tell them that there won't be any recriminations if someone has made a mistake. I'd rather have the stone than a perfect police force."

"I will. But I think they all realise that all bits of evidence are important and they did check pretty thoroughly, I believe, last time I asked them. But I'll ask again." The sergeant took a large swig of coffee before adding: "You know, there used to be a book called, 'Who Moved the Stone?' My grandmother was a keen church-goer and tried endlessly to get me to read it when I was a teenager. She said, that if I did, I couldn't help but become a devout Christian. Apparently, it's to do with the grave of Jesus, which was closed by a massive stone, or boulder I guess. When the disciples went to the grave the next day, the stone had been moved away and the body of Jesus had gone. To this day, nobody knows how it happened but some say it was by a miracle."

"Is that relevant?" said Griffiths.

"Probably not but it does make you think. 'There are more things in heaven and earth, Horatio, than are dreamt of in your lifetime.' Romeo and Juliet, I believe."

"Actually, Lees, it's 'than are dreamt of in your philosophy'. And it's Hamlet."

"That's why I work with you, Inspector Griffiths, so I can learn something!"

"Then stick around."

When, next morning, Lees returned to the office with the news that nobody could account for the whereabouts of the stone, he found Griffiths bent over his desk, pen in hand and scribbling in lines and circles on a piece of paper in a way that, at first sight to Lees, seemed completely random. Unusually, the inspector did not acknowledge the arrival of his sergeant, save by lifting the butt of the pen to his head and scratching vigorously.

"Coffee?" said Lees. Interpreting the lack of response as affirmative, he returned a few minutes later with two cups and placed one by the right hand of the inspector. He gazed over his shoulder to see a list of names, connected in various ways by lines and circles.

Griffiths fell back in his chair and lifted his head towards the sergeant.

"Thanks," he said. "Do you know that everyone on this list I have here is potentially culpable of murdering that Nigerian girl, that they interact with each other in a whole variety of ways and that we have no evidence to implicate any one of them in the crime? Yes, I know we haven't yet spoken to Mrs. Haynes, her daughter or the girl's brother but I am not optimistic that we will get very far."

"So, who's on your list?" said Lees.

"Who isn't?" said Griffiths. "OK, we have Amy Haynes, who seemed to have something against her - as yet, don't know why. We have her father and mother, to protect their daughter or, in the case of the father, because he has something else to hide - as yet, not known. We have the pimp, Adedayo - maybe to keep her quiet, to protect his business - or his bosses, an even bigger reason. We have the brother - don't know why exactly but we've heard that he is a devout Christian and maybe disapproved of her lifestyle. It may be some twisted client from the hotels - we've heard about the new trends to violent sex there. Or, of course, it may be the girl herself - suicide, in other words, although the medical records don't suggest she was a risk."

"What about that girl, Adebanke, her fellow prostitute?"

"Of course it's possible," said the DI, "but I don't think likely. Why would she come in from hiding at some risk to herself to give us information that she didn't need to give? Of the whole lot, I would put her at the bottom of the list."

"I've made some enquiries about the brother and one positive lead is that there is a Nigerian guy of his name working at Sirius Petroleum in Berkeley Square," said Lees. "He wasn't available when I went round but I left a message for him to contact us. And Dr. Haynes says, yes, we can go round any evening about six, when everyone should be around and able to talk."

"Good. Let's hope the brother contacts us before beetling off back to Nigeria. Otherwise try them again. And fix up to go round to the Haynes." Lees was just setting off but Griffiths stopped him. "And there's still the stone. How can we find it? Get someone to do a search of the graveyard. We need those fingerprints and DNA, if they exist. What was that book called?"

"Who Moved the Stone?" said Lees.

The detectives were let into the house by Dr. Haynes and directed to the sitting room, where they were introduced to Rebecca and their daughter Amy, both seated on the settee. Rebecca was seated to the left of her daughter, with her right arm around her shoulders. Amy was slouched forwards gazing purposelessly at her finger nails but she managed to look up enough to say hello to Griffiths and Lees. The men took their seats.

"Well, here we all are, Inspector. What would you like to ask us that I haven't told you already?"

"Mrs. Haynes and Amy - I hope you don't mind my using your first name - naturally, I will refer to you as Miss Haynes, if you wish."

"Amy is fine," said Rebecca, on her daughter's behalf.

"Well, Mrs. Haynes and Amy, you may know part of what I am about to tell you following our conversations with your husband, and indeed from the newspapers, but let me tell you the whole story as we know it so far," said the inspector. "A body was found in the graveyard over a week ago, very burnt and charred. Indeed, identification of the body was virtually impossible but we have reason to believe that she was a Nigerian female, not long in this country. It also appears very possible that she attended the same church as your family."

"Muonasa," said Amy, in a monotone.

"Indeed," said Griffiths. "We believe that to be her name."

"What I would like to ask you, in a very general way, is what you knew about her. Anything you can think of may turn out to be helpful, even if it seems unimportant to you now."

"She was just a normal, quiet member of our congregation," said Becky. Then, glancing first at Amy and then looking towards Mark, added: "You probably know that she was a patient of my husband."

"Yes, thank you. And we do have her medical records but I was proposing to discuss those matters with Dr. Haynes. Unless you have anything you would like to add from your own knowledge, confidentially of course."

"Did you find the letter?" said Amy with only a little more expression than previously.

"The letter?" said Griffiths.

"She is referring to a letter that Muonasa wrote to my husband," said Becky with a smile. "She found it in the printer tray of the computer in the study; that's all."

"Was that in the medical records?" said the DI to Lees.

"No."

"Was it a special letter?" said Griffiths to the family.

"No, no," said Becky, smiling more broadly. "Just the normal kind of letter from a patient, thanking my husband for his efforts. I've seen lots of them, as you can imagine. Maybe it's because he is such a good doctor!" She laughed aloud. *You don't have to be a trained detective to spot laughter as false as that*, thought Lees.

"Actually," said Amy, now becoming more animated and looking upwards but at no one in particular, "I am referring to the love letter that she wrote to my father, proving to anyone who has the eyes to see that she was having an affair with him!"

"I am sorry," said Mark to the inspector, "but it requires me to tell you, against my better wishes, that my daughter is not very well and she is harbouring beliefs that, frankly, have no foundation in fact."

"You mean what she says is not true?" asked the sergeant.

"It is true, as my wife has already confirmed, that Muonasa wrote me a letter, an innocent one, contrary to what my daughter believes."

"Do you still have the letter?" asked Griffiths.

"Possibly," said Mark. "I am not sure." Ignoring the uncertainty in Dr. Haynes' answer, the inspector asked, " May I see it?"

As Mark rose and went to his study, Becky held her daughter even more closely and looked directly into her eyes. "It's all right, darling. We know that many interpretations can be put on the content of a letter and yours is as valid as anyone else's."

"So what she says may be true?" asked Lees.

"To be honest, Sergeant, I have no idea. My husband seems to be a very busy man. He spends a lot of time away from home, apparently at work, and I couldn't possibly account for his every movement. So maybe you should ask him. As for my daughter and me, I don't think we can help you very much in your enquiries."

Mark returned, letter in hand. "You feel it important to see a letter from one of my patients," he said and, almost throwing the letter towards the inspector, added: "Well, here it is. Good luck with it!" Then he sat down abruptly in the chair furthest away from the settee where his wife and daughter were seated.

Griffiths studied the content of the letter, with Lees looking over his shoulder.

"Dear Mark,

I hope you do not mind me writing to you but sometimes it is easier to put one's thoughts on paper than to speak them to someone's face.

I just wanted to say how much our times together have meant to me. From the first time we met, I have felt a strong sense that you would create something in my wellbeing much stronger than I could have expected when I booked that appointment with you. I am so glad I did it. Because, although I know that whatever condition I have will still need treatment, I also know that my main route to a fulfilling future lies with you.

I do hope that you will continue in our relationship. I am not exaggerating when I say that I have gained more from you emotionally than I have ever from anyone else. Our rendezvous have changed my life and I relish each one and look forward with eagerness to the next. Together, we build something, certainly in me. I consulted you for treatment and you have provided that and more.

Thank you for wanting to take such an involvement with me. As always, I can barely wait for the next time we meet.

love Muonasa."

"Do you regard this as one of the more normal letters from your patients?" asked the inspector, looking up directly into the doctor's eyes.

"Why not?" said Mark.

"Just wondering, that's all. 'My main route to a fulfilling future lies with you.....I hope you will continue in our relationship....I have gained more from you emotionally than from anyone else....our rendezvous have changed my life...I can barely wait for the next time we meet.' Is that normal in your experience?"

"Of course it's not!" shouted Amy. "That woman was a plague on our life and, to be frank, I am glad that I have managed to see her out of it!" She stood and began to run from the room but her father grabbed her arm as she went past and dragged her back towards him.

"How dare you! Your mother and I have done everything we could to protect you and this is how you repay us!"

"Calm down, sir," said the inspector. "It's not helpful." Mark turned his head away from the others and sighed. Becky stared towards her daughter with an air of despair mixed with hopelessness. The DI looked directly at Amy and asked her to sit down.

"We are not here to upset you, Amy, and I am sorry that some of the things that are coming out of our visit today are distressing for you. But we have to ask these questions, if only to find that they lead nowhere. We do have a crime to solve and so we need to look everywhere for evidence. That means speaking to everyone who had significant contact with the dead girl. Assuming for the moment that girl is Muonasa, that has to include your family and you. Is there anything else you feel you would like to tell me, anything however small?" *Why is he taking such a gentle approach after that telling outburst?* thought Lees. *Ah, yes! Softly, softly....*

"Only what the priest said."

"The priest?"

"Oh, Inspector," interrupted Becky, "let me explain. My daughter had a few emotional problems recently, common in teenage children of course, and my husband and I thought it may be helpful if she were to have a talk with the rector of our church. We hoped that his spiritual guidance would ease her anxieties. I cannot imagine anything took place in those conversations that would be remotely relevant to your investigation."

"Those conversations?"

"She went a few times."

"Maybe not," said the DI, "but why not let Amy have her say and then we can decide if there is anything that we need to pursue further?" Then turning to the girl, "So, Amy?"

Amy was seated but the hands on her lap were shaking; her head was upright and her eyes were wide and fixed on the distance. She bit continuously at her lower lip.

"He said he didn't trust the black girl."

"Do you mind telling me the gist of your conversations, starting at the beginning and then how you got to discuss Muonasa, briefly of course. And in your own time."

"I told him I was unhappy because I was being persecuted, mostly by that black woman. I used to be happy at home but that all changed when she came on the scene. I felt that there was something about her that wanted to wreak havoc, damage to the church and our family. The rector said that he had had private meetings with her and he agreed that she was manipulative."

"Well done, Amy," said her mother. "Well done for managing to express your feelings and not bottling them all up inside! You've not been able to do that for a while so that's good!"

Mark stirred from a period of silence and immobility. "More important," he said, "is that the girl has been removed from the scene so there is no longer any need for Amy to have any worries about her. Now she can get on with life."

"It's a start, certainly," said Becky, looking satisfied.

"I understand your concerns for your daughter," said Griffiths, "and naturally I have empathy with that. But, for the moment, may we just stick to the facts - or, at least, the facts as you see them." Then, turning back to Amy: "In what way did the rector think she was manipulative?"

"Don't know. You'd have to ask him."

"And how did she intend to create all this damage to the church and your family? What could have motivated her to feel that way?"

"I don't know!" said Amy in frustration. "Maybe she's got some supernatural powers. Maybe it's something to do with that stone she carried."

"A stone?!" blurted Lees. The inspector waved his hand to keep the sergeant quiet.

"What stone?" asked the inspector quietly.

"I've no idea!" said Amy in increasing agitation. "She just had a stone that she carried. I often saw her take it out of her pocket at the services and place it purposefully on the ledge of the pew. Can you stop asking me questions?"

"Inspector," said Mark, "I am sorry but, in Amy's current state of mind, she is prone to fond imaginings. I know you are looking for hard evidence. Of course, it is for you to judge but we are aware of how much this girl has distressed our daughter, quite possibly may I say, for little reason. But the fact is that she has. And we have taken every step possible to relieve her of this burden. The girl is now gone, which obviously is tragic but, dare I say, hopefully a relief for our daughter. As for supernatural powers and something thereby to do with a stone, well I will leave it to you to judge. But, dare I say again, it may not be the hard evidence you are looking for."

Amy was, by now, trembling even more vigorously and her eyes were wider. "Can I go?"

"As far as I am concerned," said the inspector. "That's all I have to ask you at the moment."

Amy stood hurriedly. "Where are you going?" asked her mother.

"To Lucy's." Amy ran up to her bedroom and called her friend. "Are you free? I've got the gear. Shall I come over?" She ended the call, picked up her bag, ran down the stairs and out the front door without acknowledging her parents or their guests.

"Better see the rector," said Griffiths to Lees as they walked down the path away from the house.

Amy woke again in a sweat; it seemed commonplace these days. *Muonasa - there she was again!* Amy believed that she was awake but it was becoming increasingly difficult for her to separate her dreams from reality, certainly in the aftermath of a fix, as it always had been - although more so now - but, in recent weeks, also on wakening from sleep. *So many people are after me but that woman is the worst. But she is dead. She's gone up in a ball of smoke. She cannot harm you now. And yet, she still appears - was it a dream - or a memory?*

Muonasa was walking home from the hotel district on her own at about one a.m. Amy hid in the darkness behind one of the yew trees in the graveyard and watched as Muonasa entered through the far gate and strode onto the path. She must have been tired at that time in the morning, thought Amy, yet her gait seemed strangely purposeful, as if something was preoccupying her and she had some plan that she had to fulfil. She'll be up to no good, though; I can guarantee that. I wouldn't be surprised if she has just spent the last few hours with my father.

As Muonasa approached closer and passed beneath the lantern shining from above the main church door, Amy noticed a reddened, curved line extending down Muonasa's left cheek, from just below the ear nearly to the chin. How did she get that? she thought. No doubt deserved it. Muonasa stopped for a few minutes to examine the gravestones that were closest to the church and visible by the light from the lantern. As she finished with one, she crossed herself and gave a short, inaudible prayer to herself before moving on to the next.

When Muonasa reached a point halfway down the path, Amy became aware of a rustling noise in the grass towards one side of the church. She strained in the darkness to discern the origin of the noise until two people came into view by the light at the front of the church, walking through the grass, one from each side. Coming from the right side was Amy's father and, from the left, her mother. Walking just behind her father was a well-built black man. All three were dressed completely in black, which made them even more difficult to see until the lantern gave its assistance. Amy gasped and clasped her hand to her mouth to stifle the involuntary cry that threatened to betray her presence.

The three stopped and stood immobile in a line in front of the church door, seemingly gazing towards her, although she was sure that she could not be seen. But could they somehow, by means other than vision, detect her presence?

It seemed that the scene continued for hours because each moment felt like an eternity but it could not have been more than a few minutes before the lantern light extinguished and the whole graveyard was thrown into darkness save for a weak light from the moon in a cloudless sky.

Amy listened to ensure that there was no further movement, and strained hard to discern anything visible, which, after a few minutes, became easier as her eyes adjusted to the blackness. It seemed that the three visitors had disappeared. Muonasa was now positioned towards the far left end of the path, examining what seemed to be the last in a line of graves. Amy trod carefully out from behind the yew tree to investigate the scene she had just witnessed and walked towards Muonasa.

223

A few minutes later, a bright orange light flooded the blackness as the ground on which Muonasa stood became engulfed in a huge fireball.

Amy was now fully aware that she was awake but no more sure what was dream and what was reality.

A broad-shouldered Nigerian man, smartly dressed in a suit and tie and wearing heavy dark-rimmed glasses walked into the office and, without invitation, sat down at the desk, facing the inspector. Whilst Griffiths finished reading the last page and a half of the summary of evidence concerning a rape case - *yet another black woman*, he thought - Obaloluwa examined the interior of the detectives' office in the manner of a surveyor considering an application for refurbishment. Lees was seated a few feet away in a chair to the right and slightly in front of the inspector's desk, in a position to the left of Obaloluwa that allowed him to examine his statements and reactions without being intrusive.

Eventually, and deliberately slowly thought Lees, Griffiths looked up into Obaloluwa's face without speaking.

"I heard that you wanted to speak to me," said Obaloluwa. When Griffiths gave no answer, he continued: "You left a message at my place of work for me to contact you. I assume it's in connection with Muonasa. I am her brother."

"Thank you," said the DI. "But why, may I just ask, do you assume it's to do with your sister?"

"Because she's dead and you want to know why. It's pretty obvious you would want to speak to her relatives, especially those living in London, which comprise me and only me."

Griffiths waited. "Inspector, forgive me, but, in my job, I am used to fairly straight talking - we don't have the time to do otherwise. Please do not play games. I like to think I am an intelligent man. I read the newspapers and quite easily put two and two together to make four, not five. Correct me if I am wrong but the dead girl in the graveyard is probably my sister. And that is why you want to interview me."

"When did you last see her?"

"About two weeks ago. We had lunch together. Is that unusual?"

"What can you tell me about her?"

"What would you like to know?"

"Where she was living, what she did for work, any other activities or interests, people she knew, how you got on with her - anything you think might be helpful."

Obaloluwa winced. "She lived in Walton Street. She worked as a prostitute. But I am sure you know that already." He looked towards the floor.

"How did you feel about that?"

"How do you think I felt, Inspector?" he said, looking up again. "She was my sister, from a good, caring Christian family. Of course I was saddened and frankly disapproved. Strongly disapproved."

"Supposing she had no choice?"

"No choice? We all have choices and we are bound to follow the path that has been laid out before us by God. Yes, we make mistakes and fall by the way but it is in those circumstances that we need to pray for strength to get us back on the right track. If not, we are doomed."

"And you don't think she did seek relief?"

"I am not sure that she did, actually."

"Can you think of anyone who might want to do her harm - for any reason?"

"The world in which she operated is populated by evil. Any one of the people that she met there could be responsible for her murder."

"We do not know yet that she has been murdered. Do you think she was a suicide risk?"

"Maybe you should ask her doctor. He might well know."

"What do you think?"

"She was certainly unhappy. That's all I can say."

"Do you know what made her come to this country?"

"She said that she needed treatment that could only be provided here. But my personal opinion is that something was making her deluded - maybe that was the illness itself. As I said, maybe you should ask her doctor. I imagine he knew her very well. Possibly very well indeed. But I also know that, if only she had put her trust in God, she would have gained fulfilment and freedom from her demons. Instead, she seemed to have become increasingly superstitious."

"In what way?"

"Oh, I don't know - little things - like she carried a stone around with her, ostensibly for good luck. Our upbringing in Christianity would never have felt the need for silly tokens."

That stone again, thought Lees.

"Did you try to help her?"

"Of course I did! But she wouldn't listen. Anyway, I hardly needed to show her the way because she knew it already. As I have said, she was a Christian - or used to be - so all I had to do was remind her of what should have been deep in her heart, that she should renounce evil and pray to God for the strength to do it."

"And if she didn't? - or couldn't?"

"She certainly could do it. When we are feeling weak, the one who is always there to mediate for us with God is Jesus. She knew that and all that she had to do was ask. I do not know if you are Christian, Inspector, but, if not, you may well have heard the expression 'Knock and the door will be opened.' But you have to knock."

"And if she didn't?"

"Then she was turning her back on her faith. In that case, she is doomed to whatever the world may offer her."

"How would you feel about her continuing in a secular world, maybe even one that you would regard as evil?"

"I think it would be better if she were removed from it and then found herself laid at God's mercy. At least then, she would not be laying up more bad deeds to be explained on the Day of Judgement."

"Thank you." Griffiths fumbled with some papers on the desk as if to indicate that he was looking for information to move to another subject, then looked up at Obaloluwa. "Can you tell me your movements over the last two weeks, especially in the evenings?"

"Working mostly. And, Inspector, if you are looking for corroborative witnesses, you only have to ask at my office."

"But you would go home for the night?"

"Usually, yes."

"Do you live alone?"

"Yes. And, no, the neighbours are not usually awake at the time I finish work."

"Thank you. I do not think I have any further questions. Lees?"

"No, that's all very clear."

Lees led Griffiths down the path to the church and held him back thirty yards or so in front of the entrance. Looking up, he urged the inspector to admire the building.

"Don't you think this is a wonderful creation," he said. "Why do we not make buildings like this anymore when it would be so much easier now than it was back then, what with improved technology and so on?"

"It's a church, Lees," said Griffiths. "That's why it was made so magnificent. It wasn't built to accommodate a load of people who are dependent on the local council, like the flats we now have."

"They could still make the council flats beautiful."

"Yes, but it would cost more. And, as you must know from your time in the force, most people are motivated by money."

"Including whoever was responsible for the death of this Nigerian girl?"

"Possibly, yes, and maybe, given what I have just said, we should focus on someone who had something to gain - or who had something they did not want to lose."

"Unless it was suicide, although, for what it's worth, the medical records don't suggest it."

"Yes - but maybe even then - maybe she had something she did not want to lose."

"Like what?"

"I don't know. Come on, Lees, let's get on with what we have to do. You can indulge your love of architecture later."

"For some, it's architecture; for some, it's the Beatles!" laughed the sergeant.

"Welcome to our church, Inspector," said the rector walking towards the detectives as they passed into the nave. "Let's go to one of the offices."

Typical positioning, thought Lees, as the rector guided them into their seats, two of three positioned in a circle, with the priest taking his place in the third. *Now we can all pray together.*

"I am Martin Shepherd, rector of this church."

The two detectives gave their introductions and Griffiths began. He decided to be direct in the hope that someone of the cloth was less likely to be naturally evasive. "You had someone who recently appeared regularly in your congregation. She was a Nigerian girl called Muonasa. She may now be dead. We are investigating all possible causes of her putative death, including murder. We need to know who may have wished to cause her harm or even who had taken a dislike to her for whatever reason. Can you help us? Whatever you tell us does not necessarily implicate anyone but may give us leads that we can pursue, ultimately to solve what is currently a mystery."

"Well, you have been very clear, Inspector, so let me be too. Everyone has people who like them and those who do not. To dislike without good reason is a human failing and we should forgive those who do it. Having said that, I am aware that I need to help you and, as you have said, what I may say does not implicate anyone in a crime - I certainly do not know anyone who would wish her harm." He sighed. "Having said that, I am aware that there was a problem with the Haynes family. Their daughter, Amy, seemed to take exception to Muonasa - I do not know why exactly - but I do not think the girl is well. Her parents are very protective of her and have not been willing to discuss with me in detail the nature of her problem. I think they feel that it is something that needs to be sorted out within the family, which is a little odd because they are both very active members of this church and have been involved in a lot of pastoral work with others who have problems."

"Anyone else?" said the inspector.

"No. There will be a few people in a small community such as this who find black people - how shall I say? - unusual and Muonasa was the only black member of our congregation for as long as I can remember, anyway. People become set in their ways and find it difficult to adapt to someone from a different culture, even in a church. Of course, we pray for harmony between all peoples." He smiled at the inspector.

"Of course," said Griffiths. "Anyone in particular who, shall we say, found it hard to adapt?"

"No, Inspector, no."

"How well did you know Muonasa?"

"Well, possibly better than many who come each week and make polite conversation on the way out. She asked to see me so I had meetings with her virtually each week for a while."

"May I ask what was the purpose of your meetings?"

"She told me she had a troubled spirit so I tried to help her, to pray with her and bring her closer to God's love."

"What was your impression of her - as a person?"

"A charming but troubled girl who needed help - which I tried to give."

"Forgive me for saying so but we have been told that you found her a problem in some way."

"No, not at all. Really not at all. There was something captivating about her, I admit, and I cannot explain that.

Something about her motivated me to do whatever I could do to help, including the money."

"The money?"

"Yes, our church, with my direction, gave her funds to help her in her everyday life, which I understand was pretty miserable."

"A lot of money?"

"Well, in the end, probably more than we could afford. But, as I have said, something about her seemed to prompt the giving spirit."

"Do you know what she did with that money?"

"No - used it for living expenses, I trust."

"Do you know anything about a stone?" said Lees.

"A stone? What kind of stone?"

"Not sure," said Lees. "But we gather she carried a stone around with her, possibly for good luck or something. It may be nothing."

"No," said the rector. "I am sorry but I cannot help you with that one."

"Did she tell you if someone had control over her or was abusing her, forcing her to do things and so on?" asked the inspector.

"No but I did learn where she was living and, I am sad to say, eventually, perhaps too late, found out what she was doing for a living. So, if it's true, I suppose there may be many people in that walk of life who could have had the effect you ask about. Sadly, we still live in an evil world, Inspector, and we must continue to pray that God will guide us through it."

"Do you remember who told you what she was doing for a living?" asked Griffiths.

"Amy Haynes, I think."

Chapter 13

The Beatles' *I'm Looking Through You* played across the office as Lees entered.

"You usually reserve your strange taste in music for the car," he said. "What's brought it into the workplace?"

"I thought it might inspire me to search through what we have been told by all these characters to get to some notion of the truth. Your choice, Eminem, I find less conducive to thought."

"Actually, I don't much like Eminem. Vanilla Ice? Now you're talking! And no, Inspector Griffiths, it's not an ice cream. Anyway, let's get serious. We've interviewed all the key players now. What's your take on it all?"

"Sadly, much the same as before," said Griffiths. "Since you ask," he continued, waving a sheet of paper in Lees' face, "I have the list of possible suspects right here in front of me. I have just been studying it again."

"And?" said the sergeant.

"OK. Let's take the brothel. There's Adedayo, who runs the joint. We know from what Adebanke, her friend, told us that Muonasa may well have been desperate to get out of prostitution."

"That wouldn't have gone down well with our Adedayo, first because he didn't want his cover blown - as if we didn't know what was going on there anyway - and, second, because it would cut the income of the business, if you'd like to call it that. Then, maybe even more important are the guys that control him - the whole operation that brings the innocent girls over from Nigeria and dupes them into their nasty trade.

But, without involvement of the government and international cooperation, we're not likely to catch them. And, to date, the powers that be are not interested."

"There's also Adebanke but, as I have said before, unless she is very clever, I think we can discount her."

"Then we come to the brother. A devout Christian or, if you are feeling less kind, a religious maniac. He's certainly one of the more extreme zealots I have met, although it may be that I haven't met enough. And he said that, in terms of her relationship with God, she might be better off dead."

"Does that seem likely?" said Lees.

"Let's not get involved in the inner machinations of theology, Lees. Just stick to the evidence. Anyway, there he is."

"Then there is the dysfunctional Haynes family: a disturbed daughter, who claims all kinds of things about the Nigerian girl, which, I should add, may or may not be true; a father, who is a consultant psychiatrist giving medical attention to Muonasa and - according to the daughter - maybe more; he and his wife, who are protecting their daughter from all kinds of things, most of which we still do not know."

"What do you think about the daughter?" said Lees. "Do you think she speaks sense, is mad or, dare I suggest, is on drugs?"

"Don't know," said Griffiths, "but I had those thoughts too. Without evidence and, given the protective instincts of her parents, it may be difficult to find out."

"Should we try and get her medical records?" asked Lees.

"By all means but I suspect Dad would have managed to keep everything under wraps."

"I'll do some searches," said Lees. "Meanwhile what do we have to implicate any one of that lot?"

"Nothing," said the inspector. "Absolutely nothing. They all claim to have been somewhere else over the night of the death and can produce witnesses, they say, to support their claim."

"So we should interview the witnesses?" said the sergeant.

"Yes, indeed, but you must sense that it will get nowhere. For a start, the Haynes say that Amy is almost always at home although, amazingly, she seemed to have gone out the evening we were there. Unusual, very unusual, would no doubt be the response of the parents. The brother is always at work, he says, and he will surely get someone to support him in that, especially if he and they are involved in dodgy dealings between here and Nigeria. On that point, I have found out that he was questioned some months ago by his bosses about 'uncertain transactions' as they put it between the two countries. Odd for a devout Christian, I would say. Adedayo? Well, little doubt he could get one of his slaves to back up that he was in the house the whole time."

"So how can we proceed?"

"We have to find the stone. There must be fingerprint, DNA or other evidence on that thing to show who, apart from Muonasa, handled it. And, if they moved it, then why? They would have to be a key suspect. At the very least, it would give us much more ammunition in interview with them and whatever may come from that interview."

"Then we'll keep looking," said Lees.

As Lees left the office, the 60s compilation CD had moved on to Billy J Kramer's *Do You Want to Know a Secret?* Griffiths turned off the player. *Not helpful,* he thought.

There was ten minutes to go before the start of the service so most of the congregation were gathered outside the church, taking advantage of the sunshine and blue skies. It had been a difficult decision for the rector but he had consulted widely amongst his parishioners and, although opinion varied widely, he regarded the most cogent arguments as those that stemmed from what he saw as a Christian perspective. There was no doubt that some members of the congregation had taken exception to Muonasa - some because she seemed to have upset Amy Haynes; some because she worked in prostitution; some because she was "different"; and some for no discernible reason at all, at least none that they were prepared to admit. Thus, it had taken him several months of negotiation for people to get used to the idea before the service in Muonasa's memory was finally about to take place.

But there were still dissenters - and those who, probably because she was "different", thought the rector, wanted to blame her for all the ills that had blighted individuals or even the whole community since she arrived in the area. Sometimes the priest had barely been able to contain his frustration but he did, even managing to employ a soft voice and smiles when he pointed out to one parishioner that witch-hunting had not really been acceptable in this country for at least two hundred years. The most popular situation to blame on Muonasa was the state of the graveyard.

Even now, as they wandered around the graveyard before the service, some parishioners were in earnest conversation about what seemed to be going on around them and what the diocese was going to do about it. The churchwarden moved over to a group of women gazing into a large depression in the otherwise level turf around it, into which one of the old headstones had collapsed and crumbled.

"And it's not as if this were the only one," said a middle-aged lady in a fitted blue suit. "Just look around. Five or maybe six graves are in a similar state. Every week that goes by sees another grave heading the same way and nobody seems to be doing anything about it. In my opinion, if this carries on, it won't be long before the whole graveyard has collapsed into the earth and then what? Will our lovely old church go the same way? It might be my imagination but there is a crack in the east wall that I don't remember having seen before. Maybe that's just the start."

"Hello Sally, Rebecca, ladies," said Patricia Peters. "Lovely day, isn't it? I couldn't help but hear what you were just saying, Sally, and I would just like to reassure you that we are dealing with this unexpected subsidence. The engineers have already inspected the site and done soundings, or whatever they do. The good news is that, apart from some non-specific vibrations, they cannot identify any subterranean problem that could lead to widespread damage to the graveyard or the church so, in that respect, what has happened so far is a bit of a mystery. But equally, because there seems to be no fundamental problem, they feel confident that they will be able to repair all the damage and it is unlikely to recur in the future."

"But how can we be sure," said Sally, "especially if we don't know what has caused it in the first place? It's not as if it all happened in one go, as if it were the result of some one-off, like a freak storm or something. It just continues month after month. Why shouldn't it just carry on?   And what are these so-called 'non-specific vibrations'?"

"All we can do," said Patricia, "is be guided by the experts and by the technology. What else do you suggest?"

"I don't know but what I do know is that this has all happened since that Nigerian girl came into our midst.   We never had any problem before!"

"Even if what you imply is true, Sally, that Muonasa is somehow responsible, which I very much doubt, let me remind you that she is no longer with us so how could she continue to have an influence?   And we have all agreed to meet to pray for her, which is why we are here this morning. Come on; the service is about to start!"

They all filed respectfully into church and took their usual places in the pews. After singing the hymn, "The Day Thou Gavest Lord Has Ended", the rector introduced the service. He began by explaining that this was not a funeral service as such but one particularly devoted to a person, Muonasa, who latterly had been a faithful member of their congregation and seemed to have died in extraordinary circumstances.   Even now, he said, the exact circumstances remained a mystery, all the more tragic because it had taken place in the grounds of one of their fellow churches.

But he also reminded them that the introductory hymn, although commonly used at funeral services, has a meaning far beyond that limited purpose. He spoke all the words of the hymn out loud:

The day thou gavest, Lord, is ended,
The darkness falls at thy behest;
To thee our morning hymns ascended,

Thy praise shall sanctify our rest.

We thank thee that thy Church unsleeping,
While earth rolls onward into light,
Through all the world her watch is keeping,
And rests not now by day or night.

As o'er each continent and island
The dawn leads on another day,
The voice of prayer is never silent,
Nor dies the strain of praise away.

The sun that bids us rest is waking
Our brethren 'neath the western sky,
And hour by hour fresh lips are making
Thy wondrous doings heard on high.

So be it, Lord; thy throne shall never,
Like earth's proud empires, pass away;
Thy Kingdom stands, and grows for ever,
'Til all thy creatures own thy sway.

He pointed out that the words meant that the Christian church was always active in all quarters of the earth and that prayers were the way forward. God's will would never be surpassed and justifiably should always be praised.

They moved on to the prayers, which mostly centred around wishing that Muonasa rested in peace. However, the rector also took the opportunity, much to the satisfaction of some of the more troublesome members of the congregation, to pray that God would provide guidance or intervene to prevent what seemed to be an ongoing destruction of their graveyard and possibly even the church, for whatever reason underlay it all.

By the end of the service, all members of the congregation felt united and they left in good spirits, once again optimistic.

Chapter 14

My dear Sarah,

Do you remember the case of the burnt body in the graveyard? I imagine, like most of us, you could scarcely forget although technically the case went very quiet when the police reached an impasse in their investigation. Although nearly a year has now passed, something extraordinary has happened, which it is tempting to suggest has some relevance to the bizarre circumstances of that time.

The other day, I was contacted by Detective Inspector Steve Griffiths, who you may recall worked assiduously but sadly unsuccessfully on the original case. As you know, the police have always been very open with the press as events unfolded because they were keen to maximise the publicity, hoping that the otherwise absent clues would somehow surface from the general public. Well, things do not seem to have changed.

The inspector told me that repair work is being undertaken to the headstones in the graveyard of the church attended by the Nigerian girl. For some months now, one particular area of the graveyard appears to have been subject to subsidence, at least in so far as the graves in that particular area have sunk into the ground and the headstones have collapsed. That in itself is something of a mystery because there are no mines or other caverns known to be beneath the surface into which the graves could have collapsed and the rest of the graveyard is intact.

However, I digress; back to my main point: One of the workmen on the site discovered a stone, half buried in earth and half covered by thick foliage from a shrub that had overgrown over one of the graves. It attracted his attention because it was decorated. He was smart enough to remember that a stone had been present at the original scene of death, albeit in a different graveyard, and took it to his boss, who, in turn, took it to the police. Interestingly, the stone was situated almost exactly in the centre of the area of collapsed graves, which seemed to radiate out from it in a circular pattern. In other words, there is a circular area of damaged graves and the stone was found at its centre. Sorry, I digress again.

The stone was a very similar size and shape to that which was found by the body when the police first arrived on the death scene a year or so ago. It also had the same design around the edge of the stone. We know this because, although the original stone disappeared from the area seemingly almost immediately, the details were noted carefully by a detective constable, keen to document all available evidence (and perhaps advance his career!) They also took photographs.

Thus far, the newly discovered stone could well be the same one that went missing were it not for one remarkable fact: the new stone, unlike the original, also carries a face, in perfect detail and colour, occupying almost the whole of one side of the flat stone and positioned perfectly within the design around the edge.

The identity of the person depicted is unknown but undoubtedly a black male. It is obviously difficult to be certain but the best guess is that he is African. Beyond that, there are few ideas. Obviously, given what is suspected about the dead girl, he may well be Nigerian.

I wondered if you could help? I enclose a photograph of the stone, which I will supplement with what I see as the key features of his appearance and what he seemed to be wearing, based upon my best efforts and the information conveyed to me. Please could you sift through the anthropological archives of your brain (and, if necessary, your office) and come up with a viable solution? The police are obviously consulting experts over here but you may now have the combined advantages of working in a specialist anthropological unit based in Africa and having a DSc based upon a life time's work on African culture! Well, I hope so.

You may have your own interpretation but the key features seem to be black skin, fleshy features, longish hair, styled perhaps in ringlets (it is difficult to tell because the hair only intrudes partially into the edges of the picture) and a hat or head bandage in white (again only the edge can be seen). The face is otherwise nondescript although there do appear to be some scars over the cheeks - do they indicate that he was some form of warrior?

Any thoughts on this extraordinary case would be most welcome.

Yours ever,

Julian

Dear Sarah,

Your letter virtually coincided with my receipt of further information from the School of African and Oriental Studies here in London, which I am sure you know well. I am delighted that you are both in agreement.

Thank you for your efforts. I hope you do not feel that they were a waste of time, given the response from SOAS, because I always feel uncomfortable seeking sole views from a local centre of excellence. They naturally assume an overriding authority and it becomes difficult to argue with them, if new evidence comes to light to cast doubt on their opinion. That is especially so as they tend to "file the case away" once an opinion has been given and are unwilling to reopen it, and hence reconsider their views when later asked to do so. Not that I am levelling anything against SOAS - they are just my observations in general.

Anyway, enough of my meanderings! I did wonder whether the white bandage-looking area could have been the edge of a hat and it all becomes clear when one knows (as, with your help, I now do) that simple white hats are often worn by Nigerian men. As you say, the hairstyle and style of jewellery fit too. But the clinch was the facial scars - how silly of me not to think that they could be tribal markings! When you know, it is obvious. I have since found in the literature many photographs of people of the Nigerian Yoruba tribe who sport facial markings very similar to our unidentified man.

So who is he? Well, we may never know but the police have decided to look further into it because the case of the burnt body remains unsolved and the similarity of this stone to the one that was found at the site of the body (and later disappeared) suggests it may be a relevant find.

I hope things continue to go well for you. As I tell you repeatedly, I was sad when you left the UK but things seem to have worked out and I am confident you will return soon. In the meantime, I will make every effort to take another trip to Africa to see you. Perhaps all this new evidence could act as a catalyst - and I may need to consult you for further opinion!

Love always,

Julian

My dear Sarah,

You know me well enough to realise that I am not prone to exaggeration or flights of fancy and you have therefore been generous enough not to suggest that the events of late, related in my recent letters, are figments of my imagination. I thank you, dear sister, for that. But I fear that what I am about to relate would test your powers of confidence in me, were it not for the fact that I can support my contentions with scientific evidence. Thus bear with me with your usual kindness as I recount the latest developments in this torrid saga.

The latest facts are simply these: the stone that was found in the graveyard, as you know, bore the face of a man of probable African descent. Your own analysis and that of the experts here were in agreement in concluding that he was (or is) Nigerian.

Wonder enough, as we may, how the picture was implanted there in the first place. Bear in mind that there was no sign of decay or deformation of the image despite its having lain in the ground for who knows how long but certainly sufficient for the stone to be liberally covered with moss and lichen and to show weathering over its outer edges.

Now I know the reason for this extraordinary preservation of art, if one may call it that in such a macabre context: the portrait is an integral part of the stone. The features - the dark brown eyes, pink lips - all of them - are formed from crystals within the stone, with just the right colouring and arrangement to produce the unmistakeable picture of the face of a middle-aged man. Even the individual hairs of his eyebrows comprise fine dark filaments of crystal. Moreover, the geological origin of the crystals of the image is identical to that of the rest of the stone that acts as a backdrop for the portrait. In short, the picture could not have been added to the stone, at least not by any means that we could understand. It has certainly not been painted thereon, a suggestion that always seemed highly unlikely, given its remarkable preservation in these circumstances. Now we know that it has either been there since the stone was formed some millions of years ago or it has been added recently by a process unknown to the current human race. The former possibility can be discounted if this is indeed the same stone found by the body, on which no face was seen. Bear in mind, there is no sign whatsoever of weathering to the portrait.

As I said earlier in this epistle, even you, with your unusually generous nature, may find these observations hard to accept were it not for scientific evidence. I can confirm that what I state is supported by the most careful observations and analyses of top geologists at the University of Cambridge, not just one but several, whose opinions are unanimous.

Yes, I am fascinated by this whole saga. There are so many unanswered questions: why was Muonasa killed (assuming she did not take her own life)? How exactly did the death occur? Yes, she was burnt but the circumstances were extraordinary, so much resembling the reports of spontaneous human combustion, dubious though they may be. Who was the perpetrator? The police have no evidence to incriminate any of those who could possibly have had a motive for murdering her. And then there is the stone, which is perhaps the most bizarre component of the whole story. Intriguing enough it was that she seemed to regard it as of some importance and we still do not know why but now we have these additional facts: the rediscovered object has now acquired a face, the image of which forms an integral part of the fabric, the material, of the stone! How can that be? I suspect that we may never obtain the answers but I have to say that I will for ever hold this puzzle in my mind, one that beats in its complexity and intrigue anything I have previously encountered, albeit in a long career reporting on things that one could scarcely imagine.

As always, do let me know if you have any further insights into these remarkable events.

By the way, one more thing: I mentioned in an earlier letter that the stone was rediscovered when men were working on subsidence within the graveyard, which itself remained unexplained (one more mystery!) Shortly after a service devoted to the memory of Muonasa and the removal of the stone to the secure, lead-lined stores where the police retain what they regard as potentially important evidence, the subsidence seemed to have ceased. Again, I can say this with confidence because the engineers had detected continuing evidence of earth tremor at the time of their earlier assessments, up to the time of the church service and removal of the stone, despite not finding any evidence as to the cause of the tremors. But now, for no apparent reason, the tremors have ceased.

I trust that my obsession with this business and my conveyance of it to you have not distracted you from more important academic matters. I cannot wait to see you again, hopefully in the near rather than the distant future.

Love as always,

Julian

Chapter 15

It was back in 1950. In a province of West Africa, a group of Yoruba people sat in discussion in the town centre. Some were dressed in traditional dress; others in makeshift ecclesiastical robes. At the head of the group was the mayor, who had come from one of the network of villages that formed the broader community, specifically to coordinate the activities of the group. The people present had agreed to meet immediately after the service of the town's Christian church that morning.

Most of the group waited patiently; some of the men were smoking from wooden pipes; a few others, mostly younger, were chewing on sticks, getting high. A small section of the group towards the back, all men, were in animated discussion with each other, expressions vivid, arms gesticulating. The women present sat largely immobile, hands folded on their laps and looking abstractedly straight ahead.

The mayor called the meeting to order. The men standing mostly sat down. The agitated group stopped talking but remained standing and stared defiantly across the heads of the others towards the mayor at the front.

The mayor began by pointing out that this town and its surrounding villages had always lived in harmony together and he very much hoped that would continue. The purpose of the meeting was to ensure, in light of recent events, that all differences were reconciled and the good relationship amongst the inhabitants would continue. Today, he said, was the opportunity for people to express and discuss their feelings in public, in front of everyone else, to discuss differences of opinion and, where necessary, reach a compromise. He felt confident that, by the end of the meeting, everyone would depart in peace together and the fulfilling life of the community would continue as before, even if in a slightly different form.

He suggested that those who wished to do so should make their points out loud to the rest of the crowd, who should listen quietly, aware that their turn to speak would come. He urged against interruptions when someone was speaking for fear that an orderly interchange of ideas would descend into a raucous free-for-all in which no-one would be able to speak properly, no-one would hear and nothing would be achieved. One of the men standing towards the back raised his eyes to the heavens in a gesture of disrespect. A seated man, who was wearing a snuggly fitting white cloth hat, had hair in ringlets and vertical scars down both cheeks, smiled enigmatically.

One man stood as he was beckoned to speak. He spoke fluently and stated that he did not understand why a Christian church had been established in the town when it was against the wishes of the majority of inhabitants there. The community had its own longstanding way of life, which had functioned well for generations and did not need the influx of new, frankly bizarre ideas. When asked to expand on why he found the new church unacceptable, he stated that the culture of their society was founded in the Yoruba religion and Christianity had ideas which were not only different but also incorporated criticism of Yoruba. That was unacceptable, he said. "Absolutely!" shouted a man from the crowd.

One of the men in ecclesiastical dress was asked to respond and stated, with as much diplomacy as he could muster, that he felt sure that the two religions had much in common but it was in the detail that they differed. Naturally, he believed that the Christian interpretation of God and His creation, and the ultimate redemption of the world through his son, Jesus Christ, was the true one but he could also base his beliefs on sound evidence, namely the word of God, as expressed through the scriptures. With respect, he stated, Yoruba did not have a faith based upon such evidence. That is not to say that it is wrong in all respects, he added, but Christianity was merely developing upon the Yoruba basis with refinements. "Not really," muttered a man in Christian robes, seated at the front.

"Throughout the ages," continued the speaker, "there had been revelations from God that had to be taken on board and not to do so was ignoring the facts or even being deliberately blind to them." "For example," he said, "the New Testament builds directly upon the Old Testament - it does not replace it." One of the men who had purposefully remained standing at the start of the meeting began shuffling on the spot. The man in the white cloth hat turned his head sideways to look at him and smiled again.

In the manner of an interviewer, the mayor asked the speaker to expand on some specific areas of Yoruba with which Christianity would disagree. The priest replied that it was clear that there was only one God whereas Yoruba was prepared to acknowledge that there may be more than one. He had heard the counter-criticism that Christianity also accepts the idea of God in multiple forms, namely Father, Son and Holy Ghost, but stressed that the three forms were, in fact, bound together as the Trinity. That did not seem to be the case with Yoruba. Yoruba seemed to believe in a number of gods and now was the time to reject them all, except for the one true God. "All we are hoping," he said, "is that Yoruba will be able to see that we Christians can fill the gaps in the concepts of God that they have at the moment and make Him more approachable to everyone."

A man, dressed entirely in white, stood up from a chair to the left of the crowd and explained that he was a Yoruba priest. "What you say may be your opinion," he said, "but it doesn't seem to me to be building our religion so much as destroying it. Many of my people believe that you or some of your fellows may not be interested in working together to the glory of any god or gods but more interested in taking over our culture and our beliefs; in other words, trying to wipe out our religion by riding rough with your Christian ideas."

"That is so true!" shouted a man from towards the back. Again, the seated man with the white hat, ringlets and scarred face close by held a smile against his fixed countenance, now looking unwaveringly towards the front. The mayor urged everyone to be calm.

"Well, that is not our opinion," said the Christian firmly. Another man in robes, seated to his right, leaned forward and added, "Sorry to interrupt but I would say that I agree with my friend and I would hope that the Yoruba will truly take our message of revelation into their hearts and change their worship accordingly. That is what progress is all about."

"For those of you who are able, I would urge you to read the book, 'Who Moved the Stone?' written by Frank Morison. We have some copies here for those who are interested. This man set out to dispel the supposed myth concerning Jesus Christ and his resurrection but, during his research, concluded that it was all true and became a devout Christian.

The title refers to the finding, the day after Jesus'

crucifixion, that the large boulder closing his grave had been moved away and the tomb was empty. He could find no other reasonable explanation other than that it was a miracle and Jesus had been resurrected from the dead. So please look at the evidence and hopefully you too will realise the truth. This book is a good start."

"To remind you - 'Who Moved the Stone?' is the title. Our Christian friends have a few copies here," said the major.

An elderly man in traditional Yoruba clothing, seated near the front of the crowd, raised his hand and spoke but his voice was quiet and he remained unheard until he was noticed by the mayor, who silenced the crowd.

"Please speak," said the mayor.

"I would just say," said the man, "that I have lived in these parts for many years - all of my life - and have seen many fashions and ideas come and go. The reason that they do is that they are based on no substance - it is easy to have new ideas but, unless they are based on substance, they will wither and die like the unpicked cherries. But ideas that have true meaning - they will stay."

"The basis of our spiritual life is our religion," he continued, "the Yoruba religion, that has held our community together for centuries. And rightly so for it speaks and acts out the word of God."

The agitation of part of the crowd settled as he spoke; some of the men standing sat down, others clapped; the shuffling man was still; everyone listened and some nodded. But then things changed.

"But I have to say, if you are prepared to listen carefully, these men speak sense. Everything progresses and we must allow it to do so. It would not destroy our hopes and beliefs to take on what they say. I for one am prepared to accept that the things offered by the Christians do not take away our life, our culture and our religion but add to it." Smiling and arms opened wide, he added, "Come, let us embrace them! We can work together for our gods."

Up to now, the crowd had been well-behaved and attentive, although some of the younger men had begun to look uninterested, resorted to more aggressive use of their chewing sticks, developed glazed expressions and started to become more distant. Most of the women looked at the ground, cuddled the young children in their arms or looked towards their husbands for inspiration. But with the old man's speech, all that changed too.

In an instant, the men who had temporarily sat down stood again. Some paced about; some stared in unbelief; some gesticulated; and some shouted: "You traitor! What are you saying? I said, 'What are you saying?!' We don't need these intruders! Send them on their way! Get rid of them!"

One of the men ran forwards from the back, grabbed the old man by his cloak, bent forwards and stared into his face. "You traitor! Can you hear me?!"

"Be at peace," said the old man gently.

"Calm down!" shouted the mayor. "I insist that you all calm down. Anyone persisting in inciting a civil disruption will be arrested! Our police are on the edge of the square!"

A certain calmness fell upon the crowd until a young man from the group seated near the mayor spoke up. Until now, he had been quiet and pensive but he lifted his head and opened his eyes wide. "Thank God for this man! The rest of you would do well to listen. There is one God, in the form of the Trinity. He rules our world from heaven. As long as you persist in your ludicrous ideas that God is present in the objects that you worship, you will get nowhere. How can an object hold our God? God is indeed present everywhere but he does not choose to take his home in the fabrics that you have made or the stones on which we walk and which you, in your human pride, have selected as somehow divine. God in a stone? I don't think so!"

"We do not believe God lives in objects!" shouted one man plaintively and then turned away.

"You do believe that objects, particularly some stones, may I say, have supernatural powers so that is virtually saying the same thing!"

There followed a resurgence of the agitation amongst the Yoruba crowd. Some people shook their heads; others argued noisily amongst themselves; a few shook their fists towards the front and a small number nodded. Gradually the disruption settled with repeated disciplinary threats from the mayor. The men then took to talking more quietly amongst themselves and the women began to return to their homes.

The man with the white hat and facial scars remained seated, looking towards the Christian clerics with an air of passive defiance. His persistent smile then dropped slightly and his gaze became more intense. "Our religion will not be beaten down by your new-found Christian ideas," he said to no-one. "Our gods will protect us and, yes, where necessary will indeed give us power through the stones. I will prove it and so will the generations after me! If you want to declare war on us, so be it. You and your followers may live to regret this day."

He gazed upwards towards the sky. Two large, dense, white cumulus clouds separated to the sound of thunder to reveal a bright red light. Silhouetted against it was a Yoruba man. In his extended right hand was a double-headed axe; his left systematically dropped stones to earth through the gap in the clouds. A silence fell across the whole group. Some of the Yoruba men present, alerted by the noise, also looked up. One or two declared it was their god, Shango. A few of those, especially the ones sitting close to the man in the white hat, saw the same vision but others, seated further away, saw nothing.

Three or four of the Christian clerics noticed the men staring into the sky and also looked up. But the man in the sky, previously sitting erect and looking towards earth, was now leaning back slightly with his eyes closed. The stones continued to drop from his left hand but the white clouds had seemed to move together and coalesce beneath his feet, acting as a barrier to any further downward motion of the stones. One cleric thought he saw the shadow of a large crucifix behind the man. Another sensed that the clouds were formed into the shape of two cupped hands catching the stones. But others saw nothing.

The confusion caused by the imagery, combined with the different experiences of different people, led to restlessness and a sense of confusion in the crowd. Some of the Yoruba men began pacing about aimlessly; others raised their hands to the sky. Many of the women cried and the few children present screamed. The Christians turned their gaze away from the sky and bowed their heads in prayer.

After several minutes, the noise and light abated; the sun shone and the clouds returned to their earlier position. The major hurriedly called an end to the meeting and the crowd scurried away in silence. Except for one man - the man in the white hat, who remained seated, smiling. He cast his eyes towards the horizon where, after a few moments, he experienced a vision of a church and graveyard, in which some people were standing talking after a service. He concentrated hard on the content of the vision and soon the church building and gravestones began to crumble. But the people showed no reaction. A couple of minutes later, they were all engulfed in a spontaneous, huge fireball.

"Who moved the stone, did he say?" said the man to no-one. And, with increasing laughter, "Who indeed? And who cares what happened two thousand years ago? Ha! Well, let's see who controls the stones now! Yes, just wait and see; wait and see!"

Epilogue

In a small town in southern Nigeria, a young girl was seated opposite a middle-aged man in traditional Nigerian dress. She told him that, for no obvious reason, she had become anxious about her way of life. Despite being a strong Anglican Christian, she had recently felt drawn to seek help from the faith and culture, Yoruba, on which her family's way of life was originally based, some generations previously. Although convinced of the sense of her current course of action, she remained puzzled as to what had drawn her to this solution.

The man stared deep into her eyes for several minutes, sighed and then pronounced that she was possessed by an evil spirit that had imparted to her a serious mental disease. He told her that the only way to be free of the spirit, and its accompanying disease, was to seek treatment from a British doctor. The Nigerian would instil into her body a kindly spirit that would assist her through the process of recovery. However, she also required exorcism of the bad spirit for the kind spirit to do its work. The nature of the spirit meant that it had to be removed by an Anglican priest and only those in Britain, the home of the faith, were sufficiently in touch with the spirit world to do the job effectively.

It was essential that she carried out the instructions of the kind spirit. If she refused, took a different course or told anyone about it, the spirit would rise up in anger and destroy her. However, if she obeyed, she would be cured and could return home, deeply fulfilled.

He calmed her worries about how the trip would be financed by telling her that he would arrange a loan from his friends. He had a contact in Britain who would guarantee work for her and she could repay the loan from her earnings. He also indicated that he would arrange the necessary papers for her.

The young Nigerian girl agreed. A short time later, the man's work was complete and, on a table next to the girl, lay a leather pouch containing samples of her finger nails and pubic hair. In her right hand was a decorated stone that she had found in the countryside near to the town, a few weeks earlier, and which she had kept for good luck. She was ready for her trip abroad.

Meanwhile, in the Church of St. Stephen, Camden, London, the congregation pledged their allegiance to Christ in recital of the creed and, in a town deep in South-West Nigeria, a baby girl was baptised into the Christian faith.